The Moorfoot Tales:

Lost Myths from Scotland

Thanks so much
Steve xxx

This book is dedicated to Pauline McCabe, my wonderful Mum. A living legend!

First published in 2022.

Text © Stephen McCabe, 2022

Illustrations © Lily LeMaire, 2022

Cover design by StephenMac99Designs@gmail.com

The rights of Stephen McCabe to be identified as the author of this work has been asserted in accordance with the Copyright, Designs and Patents Act 1988.

All rights reserved. No parts of this book may be reprinted or reproduced or utilised in any form or by any electronic, mechanical, or other means, now known or hereafter invented, including photocopying and recording, or in any information storage or retrieval system, without permission in writing from the publishers.

ISBN 978-1-3999-2075-9

The Moorfoot Tales:

Lost Myths from Scotland

Stephen McCabe

Illustrations by Lily LeMaire

Contents

ABOUT THE AUTHOR VII

ABOUT THE ILLUSTRATOR IX

INTRODUCTION: MOORFOOT AND ME XI

INTRODUCING THE NARRATOR: MEET WISE CROW
.... XIX

THE OUTERLANDS 1

WINTER:

MOORFOOT HILLS, CURRIE INN AND CARRINGTON ... 7

    THOMAS THE RHYMER'S PROPHECY 8
    THE FAERY STANE 16
    THE CARRINGTON LIGHTS: A STORY MEDITATION 26

SPRING:

DALHOUSIE AND MIDDLETON 35

    THE EDGEWELL TREE 36
        Part One: A Mighty Oak 36
        Part Two: Ghostly Visions 40
    THE HARE-WITCH OF MIDDLETON 45

SUMMER:

TEMPLE AND ESPERSTON 53

    BERTRAM AND THE KNIGHTS TEMPLAR 54
    THE OLD ROAD 64
        Chapter One: Aberdreams 65
        Chapter Two: The Road 68
        Chapter Three: The Three Tasks 71

Chapter Four: The Old Kirk 75
Chapter Five: The Hill 81
CHRISTIANA'S HOUSE 85

AUTUMN:

BORTHWICK AND GLADHOUSE 95

SAINT MUNGO AND THE CROSS 96
THE SPIRITS OF BORTHWICK 102
Part One: Samhain 102
Part Two: WISE CROW SPEAKS 110
THE WITCH, THE LOST GIRL, AND THE WILLOW STICK 114
Part One: The Lost Girl 114
Part Two: Meg and the Willow Stick 117

OLD MOORFOOT 124

ACKNOWLEDGEMENTS 125

BIBLIOGRAPHY 127

ONLINE RESOURCES 129

THE MOORFOOT TALES: AN ONLINE NATURE THERAPY PROGRAMME 132

About the Author

Stephen McCabe is a storyteller, tarot reader and Zen Buddhist. He has written independent zines such as *Tarot Makes Music* and *Now, That's What I Call Invisible*. He has also contributed to various publications such as *Flash Fiction Magazine* and *Tiny Buddha*. *The Moorfoot Tales* is his first book. Stephen works as an eco-therapist and he incorporates his love of myth and folklore into his work. He is also an officer for the Tariki Trust: a Buddhist charity that trains people to become eco-therapists. He lives in Temple, Scotland, with his husband Łukasz, a lazy whippet named Euro, and Kathy, a needy cat. Find him at www.naturetherapyonline.net

About the Illustrator

Lily LeMaire is a counsellor, eco-therapist, animator, illustrator and storyteller. She has supported people with issues such as dementia and bereavement and she facilitates art therapy in natural spaces. Currently, she works with victims of domestic violence. In her spare time, she writes children's picture books on nature as well as exploring painful subjects such as death and abuse. Lily is from Bulgaria but she has lived in the UK for the last twenty years with her husband, Kevin, and their numerous cats. Find her at *https://www.instagram.com/lily_artworld/*

Introduction:

Moorfoot and Me

I stand in the middle of a small winding road in Temple, Moorfoot, which leads down into the valley. The ancient ruins of the Knights Templars' chapel are behind me. In front, a long wall of stone stands between me and the forest. Over the wall, oaks, firs and cedars are jam-packed; they rise towards the sky, lush and green.

The sound of the running river entices me into the forest. My whippet, Euro, is equally keen to enter, waiting outside the wonky wooden gate and begging me with longing eyes.

I push open the gate. It creaks and reveals the forest within; a green wonderland every bit as enchanting as Narnia or Oz.

There is nobody here. There never is.

This is my special place, the place where I feel most alive, and most alone. And yet, strangely, I never quite know what to call it.

The people of Temple seem to have their own personal labels for this forest. It doesn't seem to have an official name. I have heard it referred to as *Temple Woods*, *South Esk Valley*, *Arniston Estate* (after its official owners) and *Gore Glen*. I've heard other, more casual monikers, such as *The Glen, The Forest, The Woods, The Valley* and *The Estate*, and my guess is that there are many other references to this space that I am yet to discover.

There are sensible reasons behind all of these names, but it is curious that this long stretch of woodland seems to be as difficult for Temple's residents to identify as Moorfoot itself can be to outsiders.

The South Esk Valley (named after the River South Esk which runs through the forest) is the name used to describe this place on an old poster that hangs on the forest gate. This is the official title that I prefer, perhaps because it's the only one I've ever seen written down!

Euro and I descend the winding path and find ourselves surrounded by giant trees and the small, shallow river. Suddenly, I see a small roe deer crossing the river just metres in front of me. I freeze and hold Euro tightly to my legs so as not to disturb her. We watch her slow hooves trot delicately over the shallow water before reaching our side of the bank. Her hazel eyes are deep, shining. Then, two more little deer appear from behind the trees, following their leader across the water. None of them seem at all concerned about myself or Euro standing so close to them. Strangely, Euro watches them silently without moving an inch, respecting their gentle pilgrimage without barking. *Good boy, Euro!*

This is one of the wildest natural spaces to be found in Midlothian, and yet it remains a well-kept secret. Despite my (wonderful) job connecting people with nature for their wellbeing, I selfishly want it to stay this way. I walk here weekly, sometimes daily, enjoying absolute solitude with nature.

The South Esk Valley leads to Gore Glen just a few miles up the river. Centuries ago, there was a place there that the locals called the 'faerie nook'. How did it get this enchanting name? What stories once existed about the faery nook? Who were the last people to tell faery stories about this mossy land where small waterfalls splash into the River South Esk?

Why did they stop telling those stories?

These are the kinds of questions that brought this book into existence. (I never did find any stories about the faerie nook though, so you will need to create your own!)

Temple is one of the four main villages of Moorfoot, which is an extremely rural part of south Midlothian in the Scottish Lowlands. There are three other sleepy villages within Moorfoot as well as 15 smaller hamlets and farms. The Arniston estate/mansion house is also a strong part of the area's character.

With a mere 1,200 people living across forty square miles, humans are outnumbered by pink-footed geese for almost half of the year. Moorfoot is a land of hills, cottages, ancient ruins, fields, sheep and reservoirs. (Plus a mysterious forest or two.)

This book defines Moorfoot as all areas included in the Moorfoot Community Council Area of

Midlothian. The area itself is named after the Moorfoot Hills, which lie to the south of the land, separating Midlothian from the Scottish Borders. They are part of a range of hills known as the Southern Uplands. To the north-west of Moorfoot lies another magnificent range of hills: the Pentlands.

The Moorfoot Hills look like a giant snake at rest; a long range of gentle curves with few discernible peaks. The Pentland Hills, on the other hand, are like jagged dinosaurs, all sharp peaks and rough edges. Both ranges are stark and short on trees, offering the kind of beautiful and yet slightly bleak landscape that Scotland is famous for.

On a clear day from the fields in Temple, the capital city of Edinburgh can be seen to the North, including a great view of the ex-volcano, Arthur's Seat. Beyond the gothic views of the city, the vast seawater of the Firth of Forth cools the mind. The distant hills of Fife, some thirty to forty miles away, are clearly visible on a cloudless day. It is a serene and humbling view.

North Middleton – the largest of the Moorfoot villages – offers lovely views down the valley towards Borthwick Castle, a medieval Scottish fortification from the 15th Century.

Ancient history is visible from all directions in Moorfoot.

I moved to Temple with my partner, Łukasz, in the summer of 2019. Neither of us had ever lived in such a rural place before, and neither of us have ever loved a place so much.

As a storyteller and an eco-therapist, I was instantly inspired by the South Esk Valley; my plan to research and write this book of tales based on the myths of Moorfoot came about quickly.

There was a slight hitch, though. I soon discovered that (with the exception of Temple and the local castles) Moorfoot is quite disconnected from its myths and its folklore. One local folklore enthusiast recently told me that he has never heard of one single myth or legend from Moorfoot in the (many) decades he has lived here. Not one!

Why do Moorfoot locals seem to know so few myths, legends or folk tales from the area when compared to other parts of Scotland? Is it because there are no shops, pubs or cafes in Moorfoot, places for people to share their local stories? Possibly, but then again, there are some very popular village halls in Temple and North Middleton and there is a strong sense of community in the villages too.

It is impossible to know why some sparsely populated areas of Scotland have passed down masses of folktales and others haven't, but Moorfoot is definitely one of those areas that hasn't.

As a lover of Scottish mythology, the more that it seemed there were no tales to be told about Moorfoot, the more I was determined to find them. This, after all, is *Scotland*, and there are always stories to be found in Scotland!

And so I went looking for myths. I wandered the hills and I explored the ancient ruins. I sat quietly in the woods and I listened to my intuition. I spent hours, days, months reading ancient records of Moorfoot life.

I am delighted to make it official: Moorfoot is bursting with myth, legend and folklore. Some of the stories within this book are of my own creation, based upon snippets of myth that I have discovered. Some of the stories are retellings of ancient folktales related to the area. Other stories bring different myths and legends together where there was no known previous link. In short, I used my creativity and my intuition when writing this book, which is the storyteller's prerogative! All stories, however, are based upon genuine myths and legends, even when I've used creative license to expand and develop them.

This book would not have been possible without the generosity of the Scottish Storytelling Centre, who offered me a grant from the Andy Hunter Fund to research and create it. The Storytelling Centre is a truly wonderful place that is central to the preservation and promotion of storytelling in Scotland. I wouldn't be telling stories without them. This particular funding was awarded to me in honour of Andy Hunter, a storyteller whose passion for nature was famous in the local storytelling world. I never met Andy, but the fact that this funding came with just one stipulation – that 'the seasons' be integral to the project – makes me certain that he would have been my kind of guy.

If the place where you live seems to be a bit short on myth and magic, then this book is here to inspire you. Moorfoot is a magical place – but so is this entire Earth of ours. Myth and magic are everywhere. Sometimes, you just need to look extremely hard to find it.

Introducing the Narrator:

Meet Wise Crow

Between the villages of Temple and Gorebridge, not far from the magnificent Arniston mansion house, lies Crow Wood. Here, a murder of raucous crows gather on treetops for communal meetings. They share their secrets here. They play games. They eat flesh, and they gossip.

Wise Crow is the one who listens more than he talks. He is your narrator in this book of tales. Wise Crow's role is to share occasional snippets of information that will help you to understand the context of the tales.

Folk tales, fairy tales, legends and myths exist in a dreamy place, a place where historical fact may interact with culture, nature, spirituality, prejudice and imagination. It is up to you to decide what is 'real' for yourself – and indeed, to define reality however you see fit!

The first time that you read this book, it is important that you read it from cover to back, just like you would read a novel. There is a subtle thread that runs underneath the surface of these nature-based tales: a thread that holds the key to an important message.

Wise Crow will often speak before or after the tales, but he isn't always very talkative. (Wise Crow is very old, and he needs rest.)

When Wise Crow speaks, you can trust his words.

(The following map was sketched by Stephen McCabe. The rest of the illustrations within this book are by Lily LeMaire.)

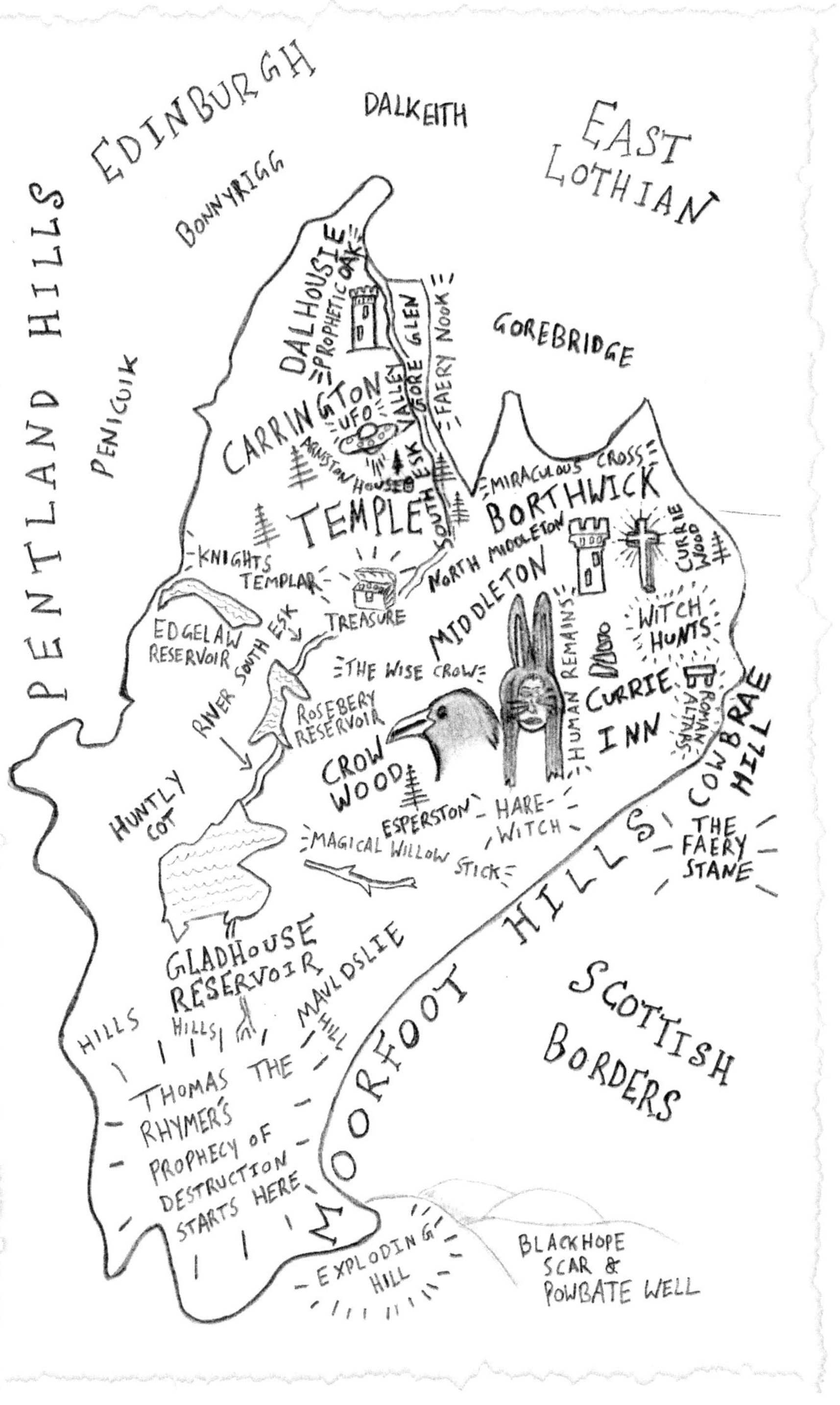
EDINBURGH
DALKEITH
EAST LOTHIAN
BONNYRIGG
PENTLAND HILLS
PENICUIK
GOREBRIDGE
DALHOUSIE
PROPHETIC OAK
ESK GLEN
FAERY NOOK
CARRINGTON
UFO
ARNISTON HOUSE
ESK VALLEY
GORE
SOUTH ESK
TEMPLE
MIRACULOUS CROSS
BORTHWICK
CURRIE WOOD
NORTH MIDDLETON
KNIGHTS TEMPLAR
TREASURE
MIDDLETON
EDGELAW RESERVOIR
SOUTH ESK
RIVER
THE WISE CROW
HUMAN REMAINS
WITCH HUNTS
CURRIE INN
ROMAN ALTARS
ROSEBERY RESERVOIR
CROW WOOD
COWBRAE HILL
HUNTLY COT
ESPERSTON
HARE-WITCH
MAGICAL WILLOW STICK
THE FAERY STANE
MOORFOOT HILLS
GLADHOUSE RESERVOIR
MAULDSLIE HILL
HILLS
HILLS
SCOTTISH BORDERS
THOMAS THE RHYMER'S PROPHECY OF DESTRUCTION STARTS HERE
EXPLODING HILL
BLACKHOPE SCAR & POWBATE WELL

The Outerlands

Legendary beings have shaped the earth around Moorfoot, influencing and interacting with its own rich folklore.

These fascinating lands can be seen on a clear day by simply standing atop one of the many faerie hills in Moorfoot and looking north, south, east or west.

Before entering a mythical landscape, it helps to explore its boundaries, to meet its neighbours. To understand the inner, we must explore the outer.

Scotland's ancient Goddess of winter, the Cailleach, was the creator of this entire land we call Scotland. The Cailleach arrived before time began, breathing a death-cold breeze into the air and smashing up the bland flat earth with her Hammer of Creation. Each hill in Scotland was shaped by this hammer, with support given by her maids. Her hags, who rode black shaggy goats into the skies at night, acted as a feminine army against rival masculine deities. Every natural loch and hill in Scotland can trace its history back to this one-eyed, blue-skinned giantess.

The cone-like hill of North Berwick Law, in nearby East Lothian, is considered to be a gigantic stool, deposited by either The Cailleach or the Gyre Carling – a local ogress who feeds on the intestines of Christian men. (No one seems to be owning up to the turd, though.)

If the Cailleach created the whole of Scotland, then the gentle Moorfoot Hills were hers too, and yet nothing is recorded about her involvement with them in mythological history. Why not? Were the Moorfoot Hills not spectacular enough to be recorded in Scotland's mythology? Did the people of Moorfoot not worship the Goddess with the same enthusiasm as the Highlanders? Or did those other goddesses and hags of the Lowlands – namely Nicnevin, the Gyre Carling and the Faery Queen – create the Lowlands instead? Some say that these figures are all guises of The Cailleach herself.

To the north of Moorfoot, and west of the massive poo at North Berwick, lies the ancient City of Edinburgh – largely reputed to be one of the most haunted cities in the world. When strolling through open meadows in Temple on a clear day, we can clearly see a dark, swirling rock-like formation in the centre of the city: Arthur's Seat.

Some call it an extinct volcano. Others know it to be The Sleeping Dragon.

Thousands of years ago, a fire-breathing beast flew across the hills and forests of the Lothians, burning the villager's settlements to destruction. Children died of horrific burns. Adults would pathetically try to defend their villages by throwing stones and spears into the sky. To be a human in those days, when human homes were little more than fragile huts, was arguably the most dangerous time to be alive in the Lothians.

Eventually, the dragon fell into a deep slumber, exhausted. Tourists now climb its body for views over southern Scotland, unaware that at any moment, the beast might wake up and begin its terror again (although it has been asleep for so long now that most people believe it will never wake).

Next to the Sleeping Dragon lies Whinny Hill: home to an underground faery community. The Scottish faeries often live in knowes (knolls) such as Whinny Hill – bumpy hills set in wide open spaces.

Here's what might happen if you stumble upon a faery knowe: a door might appear in the side of the hill. You might be invited inside by a small human-like creature dressed in moss-green attire. You will either have the time of your life, dancing to merry music, or a traumatic experience where you are threatened with hill imprisonment. You might leave a few hours later to find that many years have passed. Your partner and friends

The Outerlands

might have grown old and died. You may have grandchildren who are now in their 70s. People wear bizarre clothes, otherworldly fashions. *But I was only there for a few hours!*

As well as respecting Whinny Hill itself, ancient Scots visited the many healing wells nearby to cure themselves of illness by bathing in their sacred waters.

To the south of Edinburgh and northwest of Moorfoot lies the Pentland Hills: a range of low-lying green mountains whose mood is palpable. These hills are alive. Many are the beings and spirits who roam these jagged shapes that dominate the skyline.

The Pentlands exude kindness during summer twilight, their outlines spotlighted by rays of sunshine through parting clouds. Those who focus their minds on the hills *and the hills alone* find it easy to become one with them.

In the colder months, the White Stag roams the Pentlands. This Celtic animal of the Otherworld is said to be a misty formation, wandering through the barren hills alongside the ghosts of pilgrim monks and the skulls of dead rams.

The White Stag morphs and changes shape; his body dissolves into mist and his antlers shift to create the cross symbol of the Scottish flag, before he shifts back into a White Stag again. The symbol of a stag's head with a cross between its antlers can be found at many buildings and locations in the city of Edinburgh, such is the impact that the White Stag has left on the Lothians.

To stumble across the White Stag in the Pentlands is the experience of a lifetime, said to leave the seer with a sudden sense of deep gratitude for life. Earth's beauty is not only found in the abundance of summer days; it is everywhere, and, strangely enough, at its most tangible in the misty hills of the Pentlands during winter.

For a final taster of the seemingly endless snippets of folklore that surround Moorfoot, we need to venture southeast of the Moorfoot Hills into the beautiful Scottish Borders. It is here that we meet someone of particular interest to Moorfoot.

Thomas the Rhymer was a 13th Century poet, prophet and 'friend of the elves' who lived in the town of Earlston. Thomas was in high demand across Scotland for his two skills; his prophetic visions of future events, and his inability to tell a lie. What a combination! These skills were gifted to him by none other than the Faery Queen of Scotland, who whisked Thomas away to her underground palace for seven years. Dressed in green from head to toe and riding a white horse, she was said to have found Thomas admiring a Hawthorn tree near the Eildon Hills. She decided that she admired him too.

On his release back to Scotland many years later (although it felt like mere hours to Thomas), Thomas went on to predict some of the most major events in Scottish history, such as the political union between Scotland and England, the physical splitting of the country in two (by the construction of the Caledonian Canal).

This is just a mere snippet of the many myths and legends that surround Moorfoot. However, you may notice that there is one thing tying these myths together: a deep connection to Mother Nature.

What makes the flower grow? What lifts the walking leg? What energies bring the sleeping deer of the forest into existence? Be still, and you will find an intuitive answer. If you approach the following tales of Moorfoot with an open mind, you may well penetrate some very deep messages.

There is much to explore, my friends, in the lost folklore in this sleepy land. Much that has been forgotten. Much strangeness, much beauty and much mystery. Welcome.

WINTER:

Moorfoot Hills, Currie Inn and Carrington

Thomas the Rhymer's Prophecy

Margaret Unes is awake. There has been no Margaret Unes for almost four hundred years. But now she is lying upon the boggy hill, Blackhope Scar, *awake*.

Naked upon the earth, her eyes are slowly opening, blinded by low winter sun. The exhilaration of crisp air is filling her lungs. She starts gasping in the fierce winds.

Her blonde hair is flying wildly all around her face. The solidity of sludgy earth underneath her spirit-body smells beautiful; the damp scent of birth, of life. Three thousand pink-footed geese fly above her, honking, declaring, *we are home, this is home*.

Margaret is now sitting up, resting on the palms of her hands, her legs stretched out before her. There is nothing around her except bare brown and green hills. Not a single tree in sight. She doesn't yet know who or what she is. She is just life. The wind is wild; she *is* the wind. Her eyes rest on the patch near her bare feet: the pink of her toes, the brown of the earth, the brown stems of dying grass. She is colour. She is not separate from anything.

From darkness, from void, once again there has come colour, movement, and sensation.

The wind cries. The storytelling part of her human spirit is waking up. She notices the masses of blonde hair flying so wildly in the wind, the wisps blending with the landscape. Next, it is her hands; wiggle-bones which she raises before her face, fingers dancing in front of her eyes. Margaret Unes is the universe experiencing itself. She giggles. This is a miracle!

That sound – laughter – brings her even deeper into her human experience. Sound! The sound of (she wiggles her fingers again) – *this*. She lightly touches her face: it is round, squidgy. It raises a visual memory of pink swine. She pokes a finger into the soft flesh of her cheek. She looks at her belly flesh, and for a moment there is concern about this little black hole, her belly button, until she remembers what it is.

She understands that she is a mind-spirit, a human in another realm, and she begins to remember snippets of her past life from centuries ago. She doesn't know how it ended, but intuition tells her that it wasn't far away from this hill – and that it wasn't a good ending.

Effortlessly, she stands up. She looks ahead and she can see for miles: four great pools of water are nearby. Windy waves are splashing against their shores, glistening amongst so many winter fields of green and brown. There are spires of small buildings here and there, but not many of them. Mostly, it is a land of open fields. She sees a few small woodlands, stick-bare with winter's harshness, waving stiffly in the brewing storm like tiny brooms. *Ah remember those at least eh*, she thinks and smiles.

Even further away there are mighty hills; so many hills.

Margaret, she says to herself. *That sounds guid. Okay, ah'm Margaret, an this is Scotland.*

That is when he appears. She doesn't know how, but one minute he isn't there, and the next, he is. A pretty young man with ginger hair and a dirty face. He is wearing a baggy brown garment tied at the waist with a rope-belt; skin-tight brown trousers finish his simple dress. Bare-footed, he has dirty feet. Some kind of golden harp is under his arm. Oh, there is magic in the air! She understands that this is happening within her mind and in real life at the same time. This man is both physical and imagined.

This is Thomas the Rhymer, she knows. *'True Thomas' they called him back then.*

Thomas is gesturing to his harp with a cynical, inviting eyebrow. He begins to pluck the strings with skill. His neck-length ginger hair is waving around in the brewing storm, electric.

Finally, he speaks. Over the dreamy notes of the harp, he begins a talk-rhyme:

Powbate, an ye break,
Tak the Moorfoot in your gate—
Moorfoot and Mauldslie,
Huntlycote, a' three,
Five kirks and an abbacie!*

Margaret steps back as he plays, aware of a distinctly human feeling returning to her: shame. She finds herself covering her naked body, her breasts in particular, but doesn't quite know why.

Please explain the rhyme tae me, True Thomas, she imagines herself saying.

This hill that you stand upon is full of water, so much water, says a voice in her mind. It is not the voice of Thomas, but it speaks on his behalf; masculine, clear and deep. *One day soon, the hill will burst, drowning the entire land below, including the settlements of Moorfoot, Mauldslie and Huntlycote. Five Churches will be destroyed, plus Newbattle Abbey in Dalkeith, too. This is Thomas' prediction. That is what he is telling you.*

Margaret needs a few moments to process this. The Voice gives her the time she needs.

This is the land where you died, maiden, and one day, much of it will be underwater. This whole land is called Moorfoot now, not just the settlement below. You can be the one to destroy it all, maiden – if you choose.

Margaret frowns, confused. *But what aboot this Powbate he mentions, eh?*

Thomas continues to play his harp. He is in a peaceful trance, eyes closed and lips in a half-smile as he delicately plucks the strings.

There was once a water-well on this hill that you stand upon, called the Powbate Well, pulsates

WINTER: Moorfoot Hills, Currie Inn and Carrington

The Voice in her mind. *That is what he sings of.*

Thomas stops playing, and The Voice stops. Thomas looks at her with that cynical ginger brow again. He hands her a rough stick, about ten inches long, from a huge pocket in his dusty brown rag-shirt. She hesitantly takes it and holds it in her right hand, all the while keeping her arm over her breasts, that wild blonde hair all about her like a ghost of its own. She is really feeling the cold now, although she knows that the elements cannot hurt her.

Thomas begins to play again.

It is a willow stick, The Voice says. *Throw it in the Powbate Well just five metres to your right.* She notices a small well in the ground for the first time.

Once you throw the stick into the well, it will later appear in the loch at the foot of the hill, stripped bare of its bark by water-magic. It then has power, maiden. It will be transformed. You must go down to the loch and fish it out of the water. It will give you new powers. You will gain access to a special realm: the unseen myths of Moorfoot. You will perceive creatures and people and moments that have now passed.

Now, maiden – The Voice seems especially serious now – *if you take the stripped willow stick from the loch and throw it against this hill, the hill will burst open, burst like a full glass bottle! Water will explode everywhere, maiden. A tsunami will come. Yes, you can drown this Moorfoot land whenever you like, maiden, with the smooth willow stick. You just need to throw it into the well and retrieve it from the loch below, Gladhouse Reservoir.*

12

The stick will give you the power to see the lost myths of Moorfoot, of which you are one yourself. Once you have seen the myths, which will appear in your mind as visions, you have the option to come back here, throw the stick against the hill and drown Moorfoot. It will happen one day anyway. Thomas has foretold it to happen. Whether or not it is you who makes this happen is your choice, but when you have seen what happened to you here, you will want to.

Just like that, in a blink, Thomas and The Voice are gone for good. The shapes and sounds they took in her mind are no longer accessible.

Margaret has a feeling that this skill of meeting people within her mind might have been what got her into trouble centuries ago. The word WITCH scratches across her mind like a lightning flash: a gift and an insult all at once.

Margaret doesn't want to drown the land below, but she desperately wants to meet the myths, including her own. *Ah died here, in this strange Moorfoot land. This spirit-body o mine is a fresh birth. Ah need tae know the myths o Moorfoot. Ah want tae. Ah want tae see the spirits an know what happened tae me.*

She shouts across the Moorfoot Hills everything that she is absolutely sure of: *Ma name is Margaret! This is Scotland! Ah have a willow stick!*

With that, she throws the stick into the well – a perfect shot. It doesn't make a sound.

Suddenly she is aware that the low winter sun is gone, and that she is still naked. A serious storm is gathering, and for the first time in centuries, she is very,

very cold. If she wasn't already dead, it would be dangerous. *Ma name is Margaret,* she thinks, *an ah must cover ma flesh.*

She visualises the only clothes she can reference: a brown garment tied at the waist with a rope-belt and skin-tight brown trousers, just like Thomas the Rhymer's: a masculine maiden. She keeps her feet bare.

She takes a step forward, effortlessly with light steps. Her mood lifts. The gales begin to blow harder. The gathering clouds are almost black. The hills are bleak. Winds are whooshing violently, and hailstones begin pelting through her pink flesh, right the way through her spirit-body. She is unaffected. It is exhilarating! It is refreshing, beautiful. The universe is dancing. She no longer feels cold. She is the icy cool wind itself.

She walks down, down to Gladhouse Reservoir to retrieve the willow stick. Down to the land where she died. Down to find out *how* she died. Down to begin her beautiful haunt.

Margaret Unes is about to meet the myths of Moorfoot.

ଛ♥

WISE CROW SPEAKS: This story is based partly on a myth about one of the Moorfoot Hills. According to legend, the rhyme in this story was written by the legendary Thomas The Rhymer, who lived in the Scottish Borders from 1220 – 1298.

*Thomas the Rhymer's poem about the destruction of Moorfoot (which appears word for word here) claims that one of the Moorfoot Hills was full of so much water that one day it would explode, drowning parts of the Moorfoot area.

Strangely, Thomas also predicted that if a willow stick was thrown into a well on this hill, it would magically re-appear in a loch at the foot of the hill, stripped bare of its bark. A rural magic trick! According to Thomas, the hill and the loch actually communicated with each other.

In this tale, that loch is Gladhouse Reservoir, which today sits at the foot of the Moorfoot Hills in Midlothian. However, this would not have been the loch that the rhyme refers to, as Gladhouse Reservoir was only created in 1879. It is unclear which loch the rhyme refers to, or if it is even still in existence – a lot has changed in Moorfoot in 750 years!

Who is Margaret Unes, though? That will be revealed in time.

What Margaret Unes Saw

The following stories report on what Margaret Unes saw after she retrieved the willow stick.

She saw vivid, unforgettable visions from the past.

Ancient books opened within her mind, displaying mysterious pages.

She heard narrators recite enchanting stories.

These visions happened over millennia, and, simultaneously, within one year.

This is what Margaret Unes saw…

The Faery Stane

WISE CROW SPEAKS: In the mid-19th Century, masses of small cairns (monuments made by stacking rocks atop one another) were discovered in the Currie Inn area of Moorfoot. Beneath each cairn at Currie Inn was an urn containing burned human bones. These bones were suspected to be the remains of ancient people from the pre-Christian era. Indeed, this entire site was suspected to be something of a Pagan graveyard.

Amongst the many fascinating archaeological discoveries found in this area were two stone troughs placed upon square pedestals, named (for unknown reasons) as the 'Roman Altars'.

A few miles south and west, on nearby Cowbrae Hill, stone coffins were found next to an enormous boulder that dominated the skyline on the hill. This rock was known as 'The Faery Stane' (stone). Why it was called 'The Faery Stane' is unknown, but given Scotland's long history of belief in faeries (otherworldly little people), it is likely that The Faery Stane had links with faery belief.

❧

The old woman laid the final stone upon the cairn. Her knees were freezing from kneeling on the cold earth all day.

The cairn looked pathetic. It was a mess: flat and artless. It barely reached her child-size knees. She stood up and reflected upon her little mound in comparison with the other thirty or forty cairns in the field; so many monuments for the dead.

Shame tore through her body, cold, as if she had swallowed ice. Her little blue eyes glazed over with tears. She dabbed them softly with the bottom of her shawl, which dangled from a bow on her chin.

This won't do for you at all, hen, she mumbled to her buried lover, *not for you, my precious! It's the worst cairn in the field, so it is. The worst cairn in the whole of the land. It is! Oh, it's a disgrace to your memory!*

The soil was still soaked from weeks of depressing rain, which had at least made it easy for her to dig a hole for her beloved's remains; an urn of bones that survived cremation. She had dug up the sloppy soil with her bare hands. They became so numb that she lost feeling in them for the entire morning.

The chill of winter was in the air and although there

had been no snow yet, the hilltops were whitening with frost. It was both cruel and beautiful.

The Winter Goddess is on her way, the old woman thought to herself. *My first winter alone. Bless me, Cailleach.*

There had never been anyone else in her adult life besides her beloved, a respected leader in her community. There were no children, and she had precious few friends, although community was strong. This cairn needed to be special.

The egg-like stone on the top of the cairn slowly tumbled off to the side, tantalisingly rolling to the foot of the pile. Cold rain began to pelt. The sound of it was almost deafening, and she was soaked to the bone within seconds. The old woman dramatically threw herself onto all fours in the sludgy earth and began to sob uncontrollably.

Oh, my darling, she sobbed, *Everyone else has such special cairns here! And for people not even nearly as special as you! Look at that wee colourful one over there! And that one in the shape of a cube! I just don't have any decent stones for you, darling, and I'm no artist either.*

She sobbed on all fours in the freezing mud for a good three or four minutes more, before the realisation came.

The idea rushed through her mind; an energy bolt that got her kneeling up. She was covered in mud and alert with inspiration.

I'm going up to the Cowbrae Hill, to the Faery Stane. I'm taking something from the sacred site for your memory. I'll get you something special. Even if it doesn't look nice, we'll both know it's from the Cowbrae. That's it! That's what I'll do, yes! Maybe some of that blessed black rock can be found!

Cowbrae Hill was the centre of community life, the place where folk went to offer thanks to *That Which Is*. It was the place where the Earth was to be honoured. A rock from Cowbrae Hill would have majestic energy for her cairn.

And so, all the way up to that great hill she went, through mud-sludge fields, beyond sleeping wolves. Past skipping deer and bare winter oaks, she marched. She walked for miles and miles in the horrible rain, up, up to the great Faery Stane of Cowbrae Hill.

She had been there hundreds of times before and yet each time she saw it, it stunned her into stillness. This magnificent isolated rock was awe-inspiring; a mass of round solid stone larger than any dwelling in the community. It radiated pride. For centuries, people had sat in its shadow. They had bowed down to it in appreciation. It was the only such rock in the area, and what is more, it stood on the highest place it could stand. It was tremendous!

The old woman reflected on the mightiest warriors who were allowed to be buried there, in solid stone coffins. Lesser community leaders – yet still respected people, like her beloved – had to have their cremated bones buried in the fields at Currie Inn.

As she bowed down to the stone, the grey clouds began to clear. It was like the elements were responding to her worship.

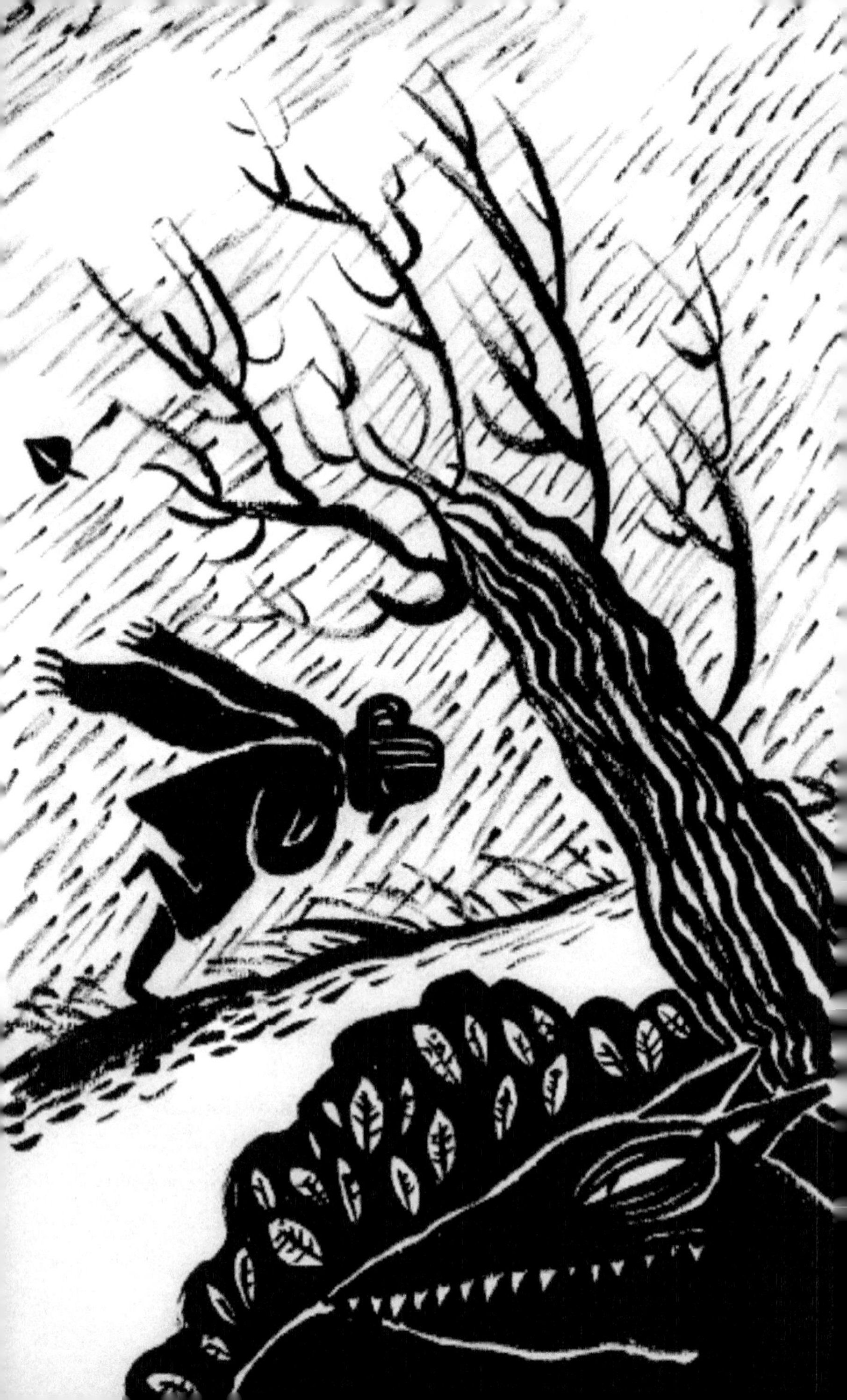

She stood back up. The rain stopped altogether, and a very cold little woman was left shaking upon a hill.

That is when she realised that something was wrong.

From behind the Faery Stane, she saw the small head of a man appear. A hollow eye could be seen blinking and peeping. This was a tiny man, even smaller than the old lady herself.

His head came more into view from behind the Faery Stane. He creepily strained his neck forward and twisted his white face and hollow eyes towards her. His features were sharp. His large nose was curved and defined like a puffin's beak. And those tiny eyes!

It dawned on her: this was no human. This was a faery man.

Fear froze her. She grabbed onto her head shawl and squeezed it with her small hands, as if it might help her to disappear.

The faery man skipped towards her like a baby fox, light and unstable. His bare feet wobbled all over the place.

The old lady had a panic attack. Fearful thrills were pumping in her chest and she could hear blood banging the temples of her forehead. She wet herself; urine streamed down her little legs. What was happening? What was this fairy going to do to her?

The little man stopped just before her. He looked up at the hunched lady. The Faery Stane towered high behind him. He put his hand into a small pocket in his green mossy clothing and with four dirty long fingers (no thumbs, the old woman noticed), he pulled out an immaculate black stone. He held it out in his small palm as an offering.

A kindness that the old woman hadn't previously noticed in him became obvious – although she still felt very uneasy. Rays of sunlight appeared between cracks in grim clouds.

She took the stone from the faery and – pure magic – immediately she was at peace within body and mind.

This is for your beloved's cairn, my friend, said the little man. His voice was incongruently deep.

The old woman was mesmerised by the black stone. She had never seen anything like it before: so smooth, and so round. It was about half the size of her hand, and she could see her reflection within its glassy surface. She rubbed her thumb against it and felt a joy spring up within her. This was definitely more special than the usual chalky rock that was found on Cowbrae Hill!

She looked up to see the wee faery man disappear back behind the Faery Stane. She caught a glimpse of his clumsy feet as he went. *Thank you, my wee darling,* she whispered.

ଶ♥

Back at Currie Inn, the old woman placed the gorgeous black stone upon the drab cairn she had created earlier. It slotted securely in place, as if it had been created to belong there. The black shine of the stone seemed to bring out the beauty from the common field stones beneath it. It was gothic and glamorous.

Thanks to the wee man, she had created a cairn for her beloved that she could be proud of. She stood back to review the cairn with pride.

She thought about her beloved: the woman who lead the little community here, the woman with whom she had shared her life with. She recalled how her beloved's wavy red hair looked when snow fell upon it, turning strawberry cream.

She recalled the times that they would sit atop Cowbrae Hill in the spring and watch the sky turn pink at dusk.

She remembered them splashing each other in dirty ponds, cooling off from the summer heat, screaming like children.

How honoured she had been to walk hand-in-hand with her beloved in autumn, crisp red leaves crunching under their feet.

Their simple life was lived together in awe of nature and its changes. They had little more in life than a wooden hut, some simple tools and enough skinned rabbits and vegetables to eat. But they had everything! Life was hard and at times they struggled to survive, but they were much respected by their community, despite not being a conventional coupling. (That kind of persecution had not yet been introduced into their society.)

A tearful gratitude for the faery man's kindness welled up within the old woman.

She visited the cairn daily from that day on. She would sometimes lay a flower by the monument, or offer some food. She enjoyed knowing that she was near her lover's bones.

At the field at Currie Inn, there could be up to ten people at any given time sitting by the cairns, silently touching the stones or singing solemn songs for the dead.

Although future landowners saw fit to destroy the simple monuments at Currie Inn, dismissing them as 'uncivilised', each person who created a cairn with their own hands understood their beauty. We *are* the earth, and we all go back to the earth. How fitting it was to also be remembered by the earth.

Even the mighty Faery Stane – that magnificent force of Nature that was once worshipped upon Cowbrae Hill – was eventually removed from the hill to make way for more agriculture. Where it went is a mystery.

The old woman never saw the faery man again. She did, however, often see the ghostly shadow of a blonde-haired woman in extraordinary dress: a brown garment with a rope-belt and masculine looking trousers. Visions of this blonde figure disappeared as quickly as they came, but the old woman had a feeling that this bare-footed woman was watching over her.

The old lady died a few years later. Her burned bones were buried in a clay urn next to her beloved's remains. A community member created a crude and unremarkable cairn of grey stones to mark the site, much like the initial cairn that the old lady created and bemoaned. *No, this won't do for you, hen!*

§❦

One spring evening, as pink twilight was beaming across the Moorfoot Hills, a visitor arrived at the old lady's cairn. Four long dirty fingers carefully rearranged the cairn into a tidy sight. A smooth black stone was placed atop the cairn, matching the cairn next to it.

The first black stone was for your beloved, said the deep voice of the faery man, *but this second stone is for you, my friend.*

Two clumsy feet skipped off towards The Faery Stane of Cowbrae Hill, never to be seen by human eyes again.

The Carrington Lights: A Story Meditation

WISE CROW SPEAKS: Reports of UFO sightings are fairly recent in Moorfoot, and they centre around the farmland areas between Carrington and Middleton. This story is a recreation of a reported event in the 1990s, which (according to witnesses) happened as it is described in the tale.

&

It was late afternoon, yet already night.

Michael's breath made ghost-like formations in the winter air. He deliberately exhaled through his mouth to enjoy the apparitions.

Michael had lived in Carrington his entire life. He planned to live there for the rest of it, too. He had never lived in the City, and he never wanted to. The quiet of Carrington held everything he wanted. The lack of people and the openness of the surrounding fields satisfied his need for mental and physical space. Michael reckoned that if he still loved rural life now, as a middle-aged man, then he was sure to love it for the rest of his life. He had pride in the place; he still found himself reflecting on the time that Carrington was named *Best Kept Village in Scotland* at some award ceremony, even though that was way back in the 1970s.

On the evening of The Lights, Michael left his small terraced cottage at the back of the tiny village. His wife Karen was becoming accustomed to him disappearing for winter walks in the dark. She respected it as his special 'alone time'.

Michael made his way through the main street to his favourite location: Whitehill Aisle Cemetery. It was December, not long before Christmas, and it was a particularly crisp evening. This was Michael's favourite time of year, and the weather was perfect: the air was crisp and dry without even the hint of a breeze. In the absence of the recent stormy winds, the ice cold air was refreshing.

Michael was wrapped up inside several layers of wooly clothing. His ginger face was a mole-poke within an avalanche of fabric. As he walked, he focused on the satisfying sound of his shoes crunching upon a thin layer of frost.

He passed a line of young rowan trees that posed on a grassy island. They looked menacing without their leaves, like dainty skeletons. He walked on past the old church (now converted into a photography studio), the wee school and several old farm cottages.

Michael had to leave the village itself for a few moments and walk on the main B-road to reach the cemetery path. The road was slippy, causing him to waddle like a chunky penguin. He stopped to admire a badger's sett entrance at the side of the road, sparkling with ice like a crystal cave. *Such a dangerous place to put your front door,* he thought.

To his right was the damaged sign: *Whitehill Aisle Cemetery*. He squeezed his many layers through a stiff farm gate, briefly noticing a shiny new sign that read, NO DOGS FOULING. *Looks more like a statement than a request*, he sniggered.

Once he squeezed through the gate, he joined his favourite part of the walk: the approach to the wee cemetery. With two low hedges on either side, it was too wide to be a pathway, yet way too slim to be a field. Frosty hawthorn hedges glistened in the low sun. The approach curved to reveal a copse of frost-dusted yew trees that enclosed the graves. It was all just *there* amongst the open fields; somehow hidden, and yet totally exposed.

Michael stepped amongst the headstones and ruins of the tiny cemetery, amongst the protection of the yews. He felt immediately at peace. Tracing his fingers over ice-sparkling ancient headstones, pondering their strange angels and weathered skulls, he felt empty and whole. He was connected to local ancestry here. It made his life feel wondrous. His mind became as still as the bodies beneath him. Within, he felt the vastness of the open fields.

He walked around the tiny old mausoleum – a cottage for the dead – reading the epitaphs on the side wall. They all referred to the old Ramsay family who had owned Carrington for generations, even back when the village went by the name of Primrose. He then considered the overgrown walled ruins next to it; a doorless, roofless puzzle from history. What exactly had this unusual stone room been, now totally reclaimed by ivy and ragged weeds?

When he noticed the first spark of light in the fields, he thought that he had something wrong with his eye (his vision often played tricks the day after a few whisky drams). He rubbed his eye and continued inspecting the ruins.

Then, The Lights could not be ignored. He took his attention away from the cemetery and looked towards the fields behind the yews and the mausoleum. He couldn't quite believe what he was seeing. The ground was alight. Not with fire, but with some kind of pulsating white light that beamed up from the ground itself. *What on earth…..?*

A vision of 1970s dance floors and John Travolta flashed through Michael's mind: a link incongruent with the crop fields of Midlothian. He watched as the fields completely lit up slowly with white lights, like a dated discotheque floor, only to then gently grow darker again. It changed smoothly from light to dark, as if there was some kind of electric flooring underneath the old crops; as if someone was gently twisting some kind of electro dimmer switch.

Michael's emotions balanced on a strange tightrope between anxiety and excitement. For a moment, he decided that it must have been some kind of cutting-edge art installation, but then he remembered where he was – Carrington – and almost laughed.

Suddenly, he noticed a large shape in the centre of the field ahead of him. It was beyond the telephone poles and before a long line of distant beech trees which were all lit up and visible by the light activity. A huge dome of light, the size of a small car, slowly rose upwards from the middle of the field ahead. He beheld its mysterious beauty; a blinding light in the shape of a perfect sphere, rising up into the sky from the earth. It was majestic, otherworldly: a sphere of light, a white globe!

Michael's eyes pained from the intensity of The Light, even though it was a good quarter of a mile away. He knew that what he was seeing was real, yet he couldn't fully accept it.

Startled deer became illuminated in the fields and, for a moment, it was a summer's day in winter darkness. The village of Newtongrange could be clearly seen in the north.

Michael watched The Light rise up from the pulsating light fields into the star-filled sky. It moved with unnatural stiffness, like a boulder in an elevator.

Suddenly, the dull lights of a large plane came into Michael's vision; its path clearly heading towards the sphere. For a moment, Michael felt pure horror, expecting collision.

The plane passed over the top of The Light, which then joined the plane on its path. By this point, The Light was so high up that it was just a small ball in the night sky; a nearby planet. It followed the plane closely, bobbing slightly like a plastic ball on an ocean wave. The Light and the plane then descended together into the airport. There were no explosions or problems that Michael could discern from his distance (some 20 miles away).

The display was over. A calm wave came back over Michael's body; a relief after being frozen in the realm of anxiety/excitement. The lights of the fields dimmed back down into their dark winter normality. Part of Michael was concerned about what The Light might do over at the airport, yet he intuitively felt that no harm would come of it.

Strangely, Michael's attention then moved away from the whole unbelievable event of The Lights, and towards the sky itself. Masses of tightly-packed stars and a perfect half-moon glowed spectacularly, unlike anything he had ever noticed before. He had never seen so many sparkling stars up there! Was this normal?

Despite the unbelievable sight that he had just witnessed, it seemed to Michael that the major miracle of the moment was not The Lights of the fields, but the night sky itself. He stood as still as the yew tree next to him. He looked so intensely at the half-moon and the stars and asked, why had he never paid attention to the night sky like this before?

Michael breathed out and watched his warm breath create clouds in the air. He focused on his breath going in and out of his body. It was as if his breath connected him to the sky, to the solar system. He breathed in the moon. He breathed out the stars.

Profound questions arose, but they wanted no answers. *What is the moon doing up there anyway? Why does it move around the earth like that? How many stars and planets are out there? How big is the universe? What IS this?*

Michael had never once, either before or since that night, ever felt so utterly at home upon Earth. He had almost forgotten about The Lights, the UFO. It didn't matter: at that moment, it felt as if the UFO was nothing more than an invitation to view the universe.

Michael did not know how long he had been in the graveyard, but he began to feel a cold ache in his bones and a pain in his neck. He slowly began to waddle his way back home.

He moved back through the strange wide pathway with the glistening hedges, shining his torch on the crisp grass. He followed a woman with very long blonde hair who was walking about ten metres ahead of him. Had she been there with him the whole time? Part of Michael wanted to run ahead and ask her if she had seen The Lights, but the other half of him knew that it would break the spell of the moment. She left the cemetery approach through the gate and seemed to disappear into the night itself, probably walking down the B-road towards Dalhousie.

Michael crouched down to enter the little doorway to his deliciously warm cottage. He went into the tiny living room where logs were burning in the fire. He took his confused wife Karen into his arms.

Karen, he said, *hen! You are a miracle. It's all amazing!*

SPRING:

Dalhousie and Middleton

The Edgewell Tree

Part One: A Mighty Oak

In the northernmost point of Moorfoot, near the former mining town of Bonnyrigg, lies Dalhousie Castle – a magnificent fortification (now hotel) whose mossy drum tower dates back to the mid-15th Century. The grounds of the castle are expansive, boasting cultivated gardens, a falconry and a pretty stream. A wild woodland area runs up a small hill near the castle's ancient garden ruins.

It is spring, and fresh life is coming forth from its hiding place. The unmistakable scent of green is in the atmosphere.

Margaret Unes is relaxing by the stream, gazing dreamily at the castle. Her blonde hair hangs heavily to her waist, the still air not bothering a single strand. Her bare feet nestle in damp grass. She giggles like a happy toddler, enjoying the tickle of grass against her soles.

Margaret catches glimpses of the past and the present, like a theatre show of visions is floating in her mind.

First, it is the 21st century. *Right now.* A long black portal on wheels (limousine) arrives outside the paved castle grounds. A woman steps out of a side door of the portal in an outrageously huge white outfit. Several younger women dressed in pink wait outside the portal in silence, holding flowers. Margaret recognises this as wedding-related activity, but it appears farcical and pompous in this strange modern land.

The wedding scene fades away in an instant. The land changes; trees disappear whilst new ones pop up, but the stream and the castle remain. On this spot, just in front of Margaret, a magnificent oak tree appears: The Edgewell Tree.

Margaret intuitively knows that this is the reason why she is here. The tree is the mightiest and most majestic tree that she has ever seen. Its appearance is as real and solid as the earth at her bare feet.

The base of the oak's huge trunk is covered in luxurious moss; the bark is dry silver with deep fissures like hag skin. The trunk grabs the soil like a hand pulling something mysterious up from underground; it meets the earth with thick moss knuckles, a green fist.

Margaret looks up where the crown of the tree meets the sky. She gasps at the height.

SPRING: Dalhousie and Middleton

Young leaves are appearing from most branches, fresh and lime.

Halfway into the sky, the trunk splits into two limbs, each section moving away from the other. Their branches spread left and right, grabbing for all of the sky that they can take. Rays of sunlight beam through the branches, lighting up the leaves. It hits her eyes, which she shades with her arm. She has never seen a tree so high, nor so wide. *Ah'm in the presence of a Goddess,* she thinks.

A man is near; a short, dirty little man with missing teeth. He works hard on the land, pulling weeds and gathering wood. He comes closer, curious, and looks up at the tree. He stands right next to Margaret but doesn't seem to notice her.

A small branch falls from one of the lower boughs. It lands by the man's feet and he flinches in silent shock. Margaret jumps: the snap is inexplicable. There is no strong wind nor any other reason for the branch to break; it simply snaps, just like that, as if a pair of angry unseen hands were at work.

The toothless man gently picks up the stick, as if it were a helpless animal. His mouth saddens in the corners. *The laird's deid noo,* he whispers to himself, *the laird's deid.*

Margaret understands. The laird of the castle has died. The breaking branch was a sign. The toothless man was clearly expecting the news, but this action, this snapping of the branch, appears to be the confirmation.

Thank you, Edgewell Tree, says the toothless man. He slumps off towards the castle holding the dry stick tenderly.

The Edgewell Tree was famous throughout the Lowlands of Scotland for many years. Those who stood beneath this mighty creature when a branch snapped were being offered a message: a loved one is dead. This may sound morbid but Margaret understands the gift in its offering.

The Edgewell Tree laid bare the miraculous and necessary bond between humans and trees. Every time one of Dalhousie Castle's people died, a little bit of the Edgewell Tree died in sympathy.

Part Two: Ghostly Visions

A blue sky appears between soft clouds. She watches sparrows flitting to and fro in an exotic monkey puzzle tree on the manicured lawn. One sparrow hops upon the head of another and then hovers above it, wings fluttering as it pecks and bullies its nemesis. The downtrodden bird flies away with a furious *twee* towards the drum tower of the castle.

Margaret looks down at her feet and notices fresh daisies at the riverbank, reminding her of springs from long ago (wherever it was she came from). She recalls little of her past life, but daisies appear to be in her blood. Once again a childlike giggle rises in her and she scorns herself playfully. *Stupid wee girly! You're here to watch, eh!*

Another twig snaps from the tree.

1695. A young woman, not much more than a girl, has died in the tower. Lady Catherine of Dalhousie had been locked away by her father after being caught in a 'compromising' situation with a stablehand, breaking that great taboo that *love should never cross the class divide*. Fed just bread and water by her disgusted family, Lady Catherine was left to die slowly, an act in which she was complicit – she starved herself in protest at her miserable life.

Although Lady Catherine appears before Margaret as little more than a shapely mist by the tower, Margaret can decipher a pretty face in the misty formation, like an apparition in an old photograph. Although Margaret is a spirit herself, it chills her to watch this human-non-human. *Am ah like this noo?* goes a quick thought, before she returns her focus back towards Lady Catherine.

Lady Catherine's ghost has been making herself known throughout the centuries to visitors at Dalhousie. Margaret is offered visions of the scenes. Hotel guests jump as their shoulders are tapped by an invisible force. A waitress drops hot tea, screaming, as she feels her hair being pulled by nothing but thin air.

Lady Catherine's ghost has appeared in countless photographs taken at Dalhousie Castle. In the middle of a professional wedding snap, there she might be – a misty apparition between bride and groom, asking to be seen. Many of her photographic appearances have ended up in trashy Scottish newspapers in the 'entertainment' sections. The misty lady just cannot let go of what she went through. She must haunt.

Her spirit has come to be known as *The Grey Lady of Dalhousie*.

SNAP.

The Grey Lady is gone.

Another stick falls from the Edgewell Tree and lands at Margaret's feet. She instinctively looks up towards the castle. A little dog has somehow found his way to the top of the tower. A woman in an extravagant bonnet is shouting, *Petra, darling, don't move!* The little dog gets a fright and jumps, not really sure where he is jumping *to*.

SPRING: Dalhousie and Middleton

Petra crashes to the ground. His little bones break and he dies instantly. The woman in the huge bonnet wails and flaps her arms around for attention. *My darling Petra!*

A dedicated plaque remains one of Dalhousie Castle's walls for Petra the dog. Along with The Grey Lady, the dog has appeared as a ghostly vision to guests for many years. The shaggy wee boy has been seen near the monkey puzzle tree, and he is often seen chasing squirrels up the muddy path towards the woods.

Petra notices Margaret by the oak tree and is delighted to see her. He runs towards her and rubs her hand with his fluffy head; his tail becomes a whip of excitement. It is the first physical contact that Margaret has had with another creature in centuries. Warmth fills her spirit-body as the dog licks her hand. *Silly wee boy!*

SNAP.

Another branch breaks off The Edgewell Tree. Petra the dog is gone in a flash.

Margaret doesn't want to see any more death. There has been too much sorrow at Dalhousie Castle, like most places, but the Edgewell Tree wants her to know, wants her to see what it has seen.

Reluctantly, she takes a final glance towards one more Dalhousie spirit, this time a man, walking along the stream towards her. She sees his gaunt yet handsome face and senses that his death also involved starvation, but that *his* starvation was not by choice. This tormented spirit appears like a flesh-and-bone human to Margaret, not spirit-like at all. He even seems to notice her, stopping for a moment to look into her eyes from behind the Edgewell Tree. His eyebrows crease as if to say, *does she really see me?*, but he quickly snaps out of the trance and moves up into the woods, slowly, sadly.

The man was Sir Alexander Ramsay. The Ramsay family held possession of Dalhousie Castle longer than any other family in its history. Sir Alexander Ramsay's remains were found in Hermitage Castle (in the Scottish Borders) many years after his death. He had been kidnapped in 1342 and left to die in the dungeon there.

Margaret turns her attention back towards the mighty oak. The gut-wrenching sadness that she felt on encountering the thin man seemed to disappear with him. It is as if sadness was his travelling companion.

She soon feels happy again by the tree, comfortable. She enjoys the fresh trickles of the stream as sunlight bathes her body.

She could stay within the Edgewell Tree's shade for an eternity.

There is so much pain here, eh, but what a beautiful gift this tree offers, she reflects.

As she watches the mighty tree fade away, back into another time – another Dalhousie – a joyful tear falls from Margaret's face and is absorbed into her robes.

SPRING: Dalhousie and Middleton

ଌଈ

WISE CROW SPEAKS: All of Margaret's visions within this story are based on famous myths and legends from Dalhousie Castle.

The magical Edgewell Tree died centuries ago, after many years of fame for its branch-snapping prophecies. It is suspected that some of the current oak trees in Dalhousie Castle's grounds may be its descendants.

The Hare-Witch of Middleton

Eh, Linda, did you ever hear about the hare-witch of Middleton?

Two middle-aged women, Miriam and Linda, are chatting by Miriam's cottage outside of their shared terraced row in Middleton. It is March 1987 and this is the first time this year that the weather has been warm enough for a doorstep chat.

A morning half-moon floats in the sky, ethereal against infinite blue. The air is crisp but the gentle warmth of spring is in the soft breeze.

Miriam speaks with a mild Mancunian accent. Her hair is black and permed and her makeup is heavy. Her teal sequinned blouse has mighty shoulder pads, giving her the look of a painted puppet. She is imparting one of her *strange but true facts* (as she calls them) to her neighbour, Linda: a gaunt Midlothian Scot in a creased tracksuit.

Linda's long blonde hair is knotted at the crown like a bird's nest; Linda doesn't brush her hair 'on the principle'. She sips a morning can of Stella Artois and offers an occasional *oooh* at Miriam's *strange but true fact* for today.

So here's what happened, Linda. And it's been proven *to be true*, says Miriam. Her eyes light up behind mascara-glued eyelashes. *There was once a woman who lived in these very cottages, ooh, hundreds of years ago, right, and she was a witch. A proper witch. And I'll tell you how they found out, okay?*

Linda nods, knowing she will not get a word in. During Miriam's *strange but true facts*, Linda rarely says anything other than *aye, okay hen, really?* and *wow!* She begins as she means to go on with, *okay, hen*.

Miriam continues. *So there was once a big problem with hares in the village. They were everywhere, bloody massive things they were, hopping around and eating everyone's crops and what have you. You know what they can be like, hares. Anyway, one of the local farmers kept spotting a particularly huge one, a beast by all accounts, size of a bloody dog. The farmer tried shooting it every time he saw it, but it always got away. It was so fast, this hare! It ran this way and that way like the clappers! Eventually he set a prize-winning greyhound on it. It gave a good chase and caught the hare, but only managed to take a little bite out of the hare's leg before it ran off again. Are you with me, Linda?*

Aye, aye, says Linda sleepily, trying to remain focused on the conversation. She scratches her tatty crown with one hand and sips her can with the other.

Anyway, continues Miriam, *around the same time, there was a woman living in Number One in this row of cottages. She was a quiet woman, the kind who you don't trust. Witchy. Kept herself to herself, you know the kind I mean?*

Och, aye, nods Linda, sipping her Stella.

Well, the massive hare had often been seen near her cottage, just over there. Miriam pointed towards the end cottage on their little row, just yards away. *In fact, the locals had seen the hare going in and out of her front door! And you'll never guess what Linda, but the day after the hare got bit in the leg — you won't believe this — the woman from number one had to be treated by the doctor for a dog bite! In her leg!*

What! jumped Linda, wiping lager from her chin, interested at last.

It's true, Linda, she had to get treated. Get it? She was the hare! She was a shapeshifter! Woman and hare, a witch! Well, the neighbours never went near her after that. Can you imagine, Linda?

Wow! (Linda takes another sip from her can.)

Miriam lowers her voice and looks around suspiciously, pushing permed frizz behind her ears. *I'll tell you something else, Linda. I've got my suspicions about her who just moved into Number One last month. You know the one, that little woman with short hair, the one who's always baking. Well, I've seen a hare in her garden more than once, I tell you. Don't you think it's strange that she also lives at Number One? And that she also keeps herself to herself? I'll tell you something for nothing, Linda. That woman is either a shapeshifter or a lesbian, and either way that spells trouble.*

This time, Linda doesn't respond. Waves of stabbing pain hit her bowels. She cocks her leg instinctively to fart, but then quickly thinks better of it.

ৎ๏

Early on in their friendship, Linda had misjudged Miriam's humour by letting rip a loud fart whilst over for afternoon tea in Miriam's house, accompanied by a theatrical raised leg. It was the only time that Miriam had ever been truly angry with her; an expression of true disgust changed her face.

Oh...oh! That is NOT on Linda. It is NOT funny. Miriam baulked. Her big earrings shook as she wafted her hands around her face. *Oh Linda, that is filthy.*

Linda felt hot shame. She looked down to the carpet and sheepishly tapped the tip of her trainers against it. *Oh ma love, ah'm sorry*, she said, *ah didnae think it'd smell that bad, eh. Ah'll get the air freshener, hen.*

Forget it, Linda, Miriam spat, *I'm sick to the core already. There's no disguising that stench with my cheap air freshener, it'd be like adding a slice of lemon to a glass of cat piss.*

Next, a look of horror mixed with curiosity came across Miriam's face: an eggy nuance could be found in the smell. *Oh! Oh, that is not right! I feel sick to my core, Linda. Sick!* She quickly lit a cigarette and mumbled something about *the audacity*.

Linda slinked down onto the sofa, deflated. *Aw hen, ah feel proper dirty noo,* she said, eyes still on the carpet, face strawberry red. *Ah thought you'd like it.*

What Linda had really meant was that she thought Miriam would find it funny. Her poor choice of words antagonised Miriam even further.

Like it? Like it? *What is wrong with you, you insane woman?* Miriam furiously blew cigarette smoke from her mouth, *I suppose you'll take a turd on my cornflakes next and wrap it with a ribbon? What do you have in mind for Christmas, Linda? A bag of dog sick, hmmm? Jesus!*

Then, experiencing yet another cycle of fart in the air, Miriam spasmed and let out a camp *oooh!* as if a stranger had just pinched her behind. She ran off to the bathroom, waving a floral handkerchief that seemed to appear out of nowhere.

Linda sat on the sofa with her head hanging low, feeling filthy and deeply ashamed. A flea leaped out of her hair. It landed on one of Miriam's faux-silk cushions.

ॐ

Therefore now, outside the cottages, it can be understood why Linda is doing everything she can to hold in her fart. She considers moving away from Miriam to let it out discreetly, but Miriam is so deep in her *strange but true facts* about hare-witches that it wouldn't be discreet at all. Miriam would know.

Linda begins to panic; it feels like something heavy is falling inside her. She clenches her bum cheeks together tightly and thinks, *Aw man, ah need tae proper crap noo. There's a jobbie wantin oot.* Her body leans away from Miriam as she prepares for the moment when she can make her excuses and leave. She clutches her can of Stella so tightly that it almost crushes in her hand.

Miriam is oblivious to Linda's pain, ranting on and on about all kinds of wild hare-witch theories, occasionally holding her hands on her cheeks in a *well, I never* pose.

Although Linda is too preoccupied to take in most of what Miriam says, she notices that the phrase *the devil's anus* pops up twice.

Finally, enough pain. Linda is about to interrupt Miriam mid-flow when *she* arrives on the scene – her from Number One, the woman who Miriam suspects of being a modern-day hare-witch.

Miriam nudges Linda in the arm with a pointed knuckle and she indicates in the woman's direction with a raised eyebrow.

The nudge sends surprise through Linda, and out it finally comes.

Linda panics and then relaxes. *Thank god ah didnae follow through,* she thinks with relief, *just a wee fart eh.* The mental reprieve doesn't last long though, as she remembers a famous phrase from her childhood: *silent but violent.*

The smell is vile.

The woman from Number One carries a black bin liner full of rubbish towards them both, heading in the direction of the communal outdoor bins. She is short-haired and stern with a pointed head like an acorn. An apron is covered with flour and wrapped tightly around her thin body. She slows down as she approaches Miriam and Linda, both of whom are inconspicuously silent for their own separate reasons. Whilst Linda is feeling fart shame, Miriam is only concerned about the woman's presence: the 'hare-witch'.

The woman notices Linda's gas. She stops and twitches her nose to identify the cause. At that precise moment, she also happens to look squarely into Miriam's eyes. Her little round nose scrunches up and down just like a hare's.

This provides very clear evidence to Miriam that the woman is indeed a hare-witch.

Every hair on Miriam's body stands on end. She looks directly into Linda's bony face and whispers, *It's true, Linda.* Her blood drops. She stumbles forward and faints directly towards Linda (who somehow manages to place her can of Stella on the ground before holding

Miriam up). The woman from Number One carries on walking towards the bins without saying a word, as if there is nothing unusual about the scene at all.

Shocked and yet relieved by the distraction, Linda holds up her friend and guides her back into her cottage. Miriam half-consciously walks on tip-toes. Linda offers gentle encouragement, as if guiding a toddler to take its first steps, *Come oan hen, there we go ma darlin', ye can dae it.*

Before the cottage door closes behind them, a bony hand appears to waft away any smelly residue.

Back by the bins, the woman from Number One shakes her head in disapproval. *Lord save us*, she mumbles in exasperation, *those two heathens stink to high heaven.*

She marches back to her cottage to continue with her Easter baking.

ᛒ

WISE CROW SPEAKS: Folk tales about witches who turn into hares can be found all over the British Isles. The version that Miriam shares with Linda in this story is a centuries-old legend from the hamlet of Middleton (not to be confused with its larger neighbour, North Middleton).

Miriam and Linda are entirely fictional.

SUMMER:

Temple and Esperston

Bertram and the Knights Templar

Bertram began to calm down after the chase. Two teenage boys had lit a fire by the tin chimney of his tiny hut. They had almost burnt his humble home to the ground; his precious tiny shed at the back of the village cottages. If Bertram hadn't been at home when it happened, his hut surely would have burned down.

Bertram was a small man with a quirky personality and a talent for the bagpipes. He was well-liked in the village, quiet – but it really wasn't wise to provoke him.

After frantically putting out the fire with water from the village well, Bertram raged.

Where are ye, ye wee bastards ye!

He reached into his hut with wet hands and grabbed his old friend; his cherished sabre from his British Army days in India.

His eyes were bloodshot. His nostrils flared like a cow's as he ran down the village's only row of cottages, chasing the guilty boys towards the glen.

He swiped at a snotty boy with the sabre. The child dodged the sword by inches and screamed.

It didn't take long for Bertram to run out of breath and slow down. The two boys ran off in the direction of Gorebridge, tripping over and crying.

It took Bertram a while to calm down, but slowly, with the burgeoning afternoon sun lifting his spirits (and a smug satisfaction that the brats would never try *that* again), he reached for his bagpipes and headed back down the village towards the ruins of Old Kirk.

He played the bagpipes as he walked, careless as to whether or not the neighbours would appreciate his music. Music was his medicine, and today it soothed his bones, cooled his rage. The locals were used to the sound of Bertram's bagpipes, and (most of them at least) appreciated the authentic soundtrack that it gave to Temple.

It was early summer. Bertram's cheeks filled with warm air as he blew the pipes, his attention split between the uplifting music of Scotland and the familiar sights of summer in Temple.

He passed the little village shop on his left and watched the street winding down towards the Old Kirk ruins opposite the gate to the forest. He looked up at the lush trees of the forest, the natural glamour of pines and cedars waving in the gorgeous blue sky. There was nothing but trees ahead and the sounds of bagpipes and the running river. Bliss.

Bertram continued to play the pipes as walked. He soon arrived at the cemetery, his place of peace, and entered through a gate in the old stone wall. He put his bagpipes down next to a yew tree and looked around to check that he was alone. He then lifted his kilt and urinated against the wall.

Relieved by the peace of the cemetery (and the emptying of his bladder), he felt his tense muscles relax. The trauma of his days in India – those days that he refused to speak about to anyone – had flashed before him when he smelt smoke from inside his hut. He acknowledged to himself, matter-of-factly, that he might have killed that boy if the sabre had been just a few inches closer. He felt as if he should have been sorry about that, but he wasn't. Bertram had very little in this world, and he fiercely guarded the few possessions that he had.

Bertram paused to admire a perfect line of yew trees that hid the River South Esk from view, digging their thick roots into an old crumbling wall. The sound of the water running over rocks and fallen trees cooled his hot anxiety.

He then approached his favourite place, the reason why he was here; the ruins of the infamous Knights Templar's ancient chapel, The Old Kirk.

The Old Kirk sat amongst numerous headstones: ancient skull-and-cross-bone slabs and gothic *memento mori* carvings from centuries past. Some of the headstones were only half visible, peeping up above the earth.

He smiled as a young rabbit skipped about around the yews. He liked rabbits, but they made him hungry too; trapping them was one of his major sources of food. *They're guid alive o deid*, he thought.

He looked up at The Old Kirk. He was fascinated by the Knights Templar, this ancient order of military monks who had gone on crusades in Jerusalem, protecting pilgrims to 'the holy land' from attack.

Bertram had never heard of the Knights Templar until he moved to Temple shortly after leaving India. These ruins were the remains of their old headquarters in Scotland. The village of Temple was once their land; the village is named after them, although it was called Balantrodoch initially ('settlement of the warriors').

Bertram looked up. The roof was entirely missing from the ruined building, but the walls were remarkably intact for something that had stood for so many centuries. He was aware that the initial building would have been circular (rather than the rectangular building that stood before him) although he couldn't remember where he had learned that information. Whilst he knew that what stood before him wasn't the original building, he also knew that it had a lot of the original materials; it was a radical alteration, not a replacement building.

He stepped into this strange indoor-outdoor space, leaving his bagpipes back at the yew. Nature had completely reclaimed the building; mosses, creeping ivy and wildflowers created a beautiful wild garden where monks had once performed elaborate ceremonies.

Bertram mentally pieced together everything that he had learned about the Templars. He wasn't interested in their actual *history*, but the myths and legends of the Templars were frightening and fascinating. They illuminated his imagination,

SUMMER: Temple and Esperston

stimulated images and stories that frightened and attracted him to this place.

From inside, he looked through an empty gothic window frame where the yews thrived.

Baphomet, he thought.

He shuddered to himself as he thought about Baphomet, the demon-like idol that the Knights Templar had supposedly worshipped. The figure would appear to him in nightmares; an androgynous hairy figure with a goat's beard. In terrifying dreams that mingled with traumatic memories from India, he would see every detail of the Baphomet's body: horns, hooves, giant wings and a human torso, half Pan from Greek Mythology, half Satan himself.

Bertram shook his head as if to expel the Baphomet. The anxiety of the village chase was returning. To soothe himself, he ran a finger over a tiny yew sapling that was growing out of a crevice in the wall. At the top of the crumbling walls he noticed a goldcrest – Scotland's smallest bird – darting about and singing. It was so tiny that he initially thought it was a bee! The simplicity of nature once again soothed him, but not for long.

Bertram's mind darkened as yet more stories of the Templars returned to his mind. He had once been told that the Templars had confessed to worshipping a demonic cat-like figure, kissing statues of it 'below its tail'. He shuddered as he recalled the details – a cat devil figure that had been *greased with the fat of newborn babies.* Then he remembered more; hadn't the Templars eaten human ashes in their food? Didn't they have sex with each other? *Men having sex together?* He frowned and recalled that the Templars were also rich and powerful, and that the Catholic Church had created a lot of false accusations against them in some kind of vendetta. What was true, and what was myth? Why did he find this place so strangely peaceful, when all these disturbing stories would come to his mind and frighten him whilst he was here? Was it possible to be peaceful and disturbed at the same time?

He was aware of sweat collecting around his collar. Today was *hot* and there was no breeze whatsoever. He looked up as three swallows passed by in the blue sky. Their black-and-white bodies darted at incredible speed, pulling morbid feline images out of his mind and taking them to the trees.

The next Templar myth came to him; weren't they supposed to have been the direct descendants of Jesus Christ? Wasn't this myth referenced somewhere in a cryptic carved message on the walls of the Old Kirk? He visualised a fresh image of the Templars: quiet monks, bald, praying to a Jesus statue, here on this very spot. The image soothed him, made him feel like the very earth that he stood upon was blessed and holy.

These opposing myths were closely associated in his mind; the hideous Baphomet worshippers and the pious descendants of Jesus. It was disorientating and mesmerising. He couldn't figure out the Knights Templar, and this is exactly why he was so drawn to them, their utter mystery. Even the cold hard facts felt contradictory – *warrior monks* – never mind the myths!

Bertram looked down towards the earth, to colourful wildflowers at his feet. A giant white foxglove expressed purity. The scent and colour of summer. Beautiful. Another goldcrest made an appearance on the stony window ledge. The tiny bird eyed him curiously before darting off into the yews, its yellow mohawk a dash of vibrancy amongst the green. *That thing is nae more than a heid wi' feet.*

Bertram breathed in and out slowly, watching his breath. He felt connection to the past, and to nature. The creeping ivy which claimed the archways offered enclosed safety and yet a sense of freedom, of wilderness. Bertram smiled at the contradiction in his experience here, almost as contradictory as the warrior monks. A baby mouse popped its head out of a hole in the wall and then disappeared back into its tiny cave.

Bertram slowly moved away from the ruins. He was relaxed, soothed, yet so thirsty in the heat. He picked up his bagpipes and made his way up the village street to quench his thirst with water from the well.

After a cool drink of water in the sun, Bertram wandered over to the wheat fields behind the little school. He wanted to ponder on just one more myth of the Scottish Knights Templar.

Glancing back towards the village street, his eyes fell upon the smooth outline of a large hill behind the cottages.

Once again, joy and fear met. Some people claimed that this unnatural-looking hill was the site of a mass grave, human bodies buried in piles. This legend had been passed down in Temple for centuries. The hill's strange, dome-like appearance added to the suspicion; it looks as if it could have been made by (many) human hands rather than by Mother Nature. This horrific claim came with no whys or hows, no backstory; just bodies.

The legend of the buried bodies, however, was counterbalanced by a far more attractive story about the hill. The very same site was said to be the place where the Templars had buried their (very valuable) treasure, before being forced to hand their land over to Scotland's authorities in the early 14th Century. The suppression of the Scottish Knights Templar wasn't something Bertram cared much about, but the idea of finding treasure in that hill was definitely interesting! But what would he find if he *did* go digging? Glistening sparkles of treasure, or the rotten skeletons of humans? Bertram wouldn't have been surprised if both were true. It would be typical of the Knights Templar to be disgusting and glamorous all at once.

Bertram smiled. He would dig for the treasure some other day. Today was for simpler things, for

SUMMER: Temple and Esperston

the drinking of whisky and for the playing of music in summer fields. He took hold of his bagpipes and began to play *Scotland the Brave*. His eyes fixed upon the smooth outline of that mysterious green hill behind the cottages as wood pigeons flapped about in someone's garden plum tree.

After the song was over, the heat became too much for him. He lay his bagpipes on the ground and took refuge in the shelter of an ancient horse chestnut tree. This strange village was Bertram's home. As basic as his living conditions were (he had no running water or sanitation in his hut), he felt that he had all that he needed. He had music and he had nature. His mind was illuminated with stories, with imagination. He had life.

Bertram leaned back against the thick trunk of the ancient tree.

Gently, he recited a centuries-old rhyme about Temple's buried treasure:

Twixt the oak and the elm tree/ You will find buried the millions free.

&

To this day, bagpipes can be heard in the fields of Temple, close to where Bertram's tiny hut once stood. Only those who are attuned to the spirit world can hear. There is never a player to be seen.

ೇ

WISE CROW SPEAKS: Bertram was a Temple resident who moved to the village from India in the early 20th century. He lived in the hut for several decades (roughly 1900 – 1920-ish). His ghost is said to play the bagpipes in the fields to this day. Jock Gilchrist, one of the boys who tried to set fire to his hut, lived in Temple for the rest of his life. He never forgot his close call with Bertram's sabre.

This story features well-known myths about the Knights Templar and the village of Temple. For historical facts about the Knights Templar, seek other sources. Remember that the world of myth and legend is not the same as the world of historical fact. You are in a different realm here.

The Old Road

In a witch's vision, an old red leather book appears. It is luxurious and mysterious, with the words *Lost Fairy Tales for Children* inscribed in faded gold.

The book opens of its own accord, creaking. The witch feels uneasy. Cream-coloured pages flicker from left to right as if being blown by a determined wind.

Titles are briefly glimpsed:

Hansel and Gretel

and then

The Little Fir Tree.

The pages stop turning.

They settle on the centre pages.

The witch reads the title:

The Old Road

She takes a deep breath.

Slowly, the witch begins to read the old fairy tale.

୫❧

Chapter One: Aberdreams

Once upon a time, in a land of rolling green hills and pine trees, there was a young prince.

In the daytime, the prince lived in the physical land of Aberdeenshire. At night, he lived in the supernatural land of dreams. Sometimes, when he concentrated, he was able to travel to another place; the magical land of Aberdreams.

The young prince was handsome with dark skin and shaggy black hair. He was also extremely sad. He was so bored with royal life. He wished to become a knight with the old Knights Templar instead of being a boring prince.

As a child, he had been told many stories about the Knights Templars' battles, and how those stories had enchanted him! His father, the king, told him all about their crusades in far away countries, wearing silver armour and riding brilliant white horses.

The Knights Templars' chapel sat proudly at the bottom of a beautiful green valley in the village of Temple – a faraway place, deep in the south of Scotland.

The young prince was born too late to become a member of the Knights Templar. The Knights Templar had been forced by the rulers of Scotland to give up their land long before he was born. Some of the mighty knights were even murdered. All that remained of them now was the ruins of their chapel in the village of Temple – and a big green hill that some people claimed they had created with their own hands. The smooth hill was said to be where their treasure was buried. It had been built so high that nobody would ever be able to find the treasure within it.

The prince knew that he had to find that hill in southern Scotland, but Aberdeenshire was in the Northeast, so far away.

But there were two Temples. The Temple in the physical world, and the other, more mysterious Temple, that lay within the realm of Aberdreams.

In many ways, Aberdreams was the same as Earth. However, in Aberdreams, magical and impossible things could happen – like becoming a Templar Knight!

The prince wasn't interested in the treasure; he was rich already. The prince had been having strange dreams, and in those dreams, if he found the Knights Templar's hill and stood on top of it, he would look up and find the Knights Templar there, riding in the sky. He had to make his dreams reality.

One day, after his mother, the Queen, had shouted at him for having smelly underpants, he decided that enough was enough. No more boring life in the castle! He would go on a pilgrimage to find the Knights Templar!

The prince took his favourite little shoulder bag and dressed in peasant rags so that nobody would know that he was a prince. He was tired of people bowing to him and being nice to him. He wanted to see what it was like to be a normal person. He wanted to become a Templar Knight on his own merit, not because he was a prince. Once he was in his disguise, he left the castle and walked towards The Old Road.

The Old Road was nestled in the middle of a great forest. He arrived at the beginning of the road between lush summer trees, and decided that this was the place where he would enter Aberdreams.

Red squirrels scurried from one side of the road to another, and the sun felt warm against his skin. The prince felt relaxed in the warmth and he began his journey.

He closed his eyes tightly and tensed every muscle. He concentrated hard, thinking only of Aberdreams. Finally, he released the tension in his muscles, said a secret magic word in his mind, and opened his eyes.

The first thing he saw was a skinny woman with the head of a pig running off into the shrubs. There was no doubt about it – the prince was back in Aberdreams!

Chapter Two: The Road

The prince knew that if he followed The Old Road, he would find Temple. He began to walk slowly, enjoying the sight of the tall pine trees that reached high into the sky on either side of him. He loved the shadows that the trees would cast on the sunny path of The Old Road. He decided that he would walk slowly and preserve his energy. It was important for him to enjoy the journey and to feel relaxed.

The prince stopped to admire a giant old oak tree on his left, deep in the forest and away from the road. He walked towards it, through masses of stinging nettles on the side of the road. He got stung, *ouch,* but he was happy regardless – it was hard not to be happy on a summer's day in a beautiful forest. He skipped over a pretty little stream that gently reflected the sun's light, and then he stopped to admire the oak.

He knelt before the Oak, but not too close to it. He noticed several purple foxgloves by the trunk. "Foxglove flowers are often near gateways to the Otherworld", he said to himself. He asked the tree for a message, sensing that it was important. "Can I have a message from the Otherworld, please Oak?"

Suddenly, out of a little door in the Oak's wide trunk, there came a dark shadow in the shape of a man. The dark shadow was a disturbing sight in the sunlight; it was as if a piece of the night sky, shaped like a human being, was here in the sunny forest! Parts of the shadow twinkled like tiny stars. No human features could be seen on its face.

The young prince was terrified as the dark shadow walked sternly towards him, and yet….he was also excited. He knew that this creature was a demon from the Otherworld. He knew that an adventure was about to begin!

"You can't fool me, young man", said the demon in a hoarse voice, like an old man with a bad chest. "Those rags that you are wearing do not disguise the clear fact that you were born of a noble family."

"I…I am on a p-p-pilgrimage," said the nervous young prince, "I want to join a crusade with the Knights Templar, and I….", he gulped, afraid of what he was about to say,"…I…I want you to help me."

The young knight knew that demons were dangerous, but he had a feeling that this demon might be able to help him on his journey.

The demon spoke again. "If you want to go on a crusade," it said, "this is possible. You already live in the correct state: you did right to come to Aberdreams. To join the Knights Templar, however, you will need to complete three tasks."

SUMMER: Temple and Esperston

"Three tasks!" shouted the excited prince. This was like something from a fairy tale! The young prince took in a sharp breath and looked at the demon with wild, impatient eyes.

Chapter Three: The Three Tasks

"Firstly," said the demon, "you must find a stone from the burn over there." The demon pointed towards the little stream that the prince had skipped over earlier. "Secondly," he continued, "you must find a beautiful purple thistle with the sharpest prickles, and finally, you must find a smooth, shiny acorn from this very oak tree that I appeared from. If you can find these three things and use them in the correct manner, you might be able to join the famous Knights Templar."

The young prince looked frightened and confused. The demon seemed to be annoyed by this, raising his voice a little to say, "If you fail to find these three things and use them in the correct way, you will forfeit your life and never get a chance to go on a crusade with the Knights Templar. You will die a horrible death. A truly horrible death, child."

The demon then calmly walked back into the door inside the oak tree, and the door disappeared.

The young prince felt much calmer now that the shadow man had gone. He got straight to work.

Firstly, he found a stone in the burn and put it in his pocket.

Secondly, he found a beautiful purple thistle from a pretty wildflower meadow. He put the thistle into his little bag so that he wouldn't stab himself with its sharp prickles.

Finally, he found the shiniest acorn he had ever seen in the old oak tree and he put it in his pocket with the stone. He found it strange that there would be acorns at this time of year, but then he remembered that he was in Aberdreams, and that he had just been talking with a demon. Summer acorns were no more unusual than being given three tasks to do by a shadow who lives in a tree trunk!

The prince thought about his three items and became confused. What was he going to do with these three items? What did the demon mean when he said that they needed to be "used correctly"?

The prince walked along the Old Road towards Temple. He knew that it was very far away, yet he felt that time was passing much faster than ever before. He felt as if he were crossing great distances within the blink of an eye. He felt powerful, and he suspected that it had something to do with the three magical items that he was carrying: the stone, the thistle and the acorn.

The prince stopped in his tracks. He saw a figure move towards him from the direction he was headed – and it wasn't pretty.

As the figure came closer, the prince was shocked to see such a strange beast. It had the head of an eagle, the chest of a strong man and the white wings of an angel. The creature was not much taller than the prince, but with its huge wings (which were spread out to either side of it) and sharp talons that dug into the muddy earth as it walked, he knew he was in danger.

The creature stopped in front of the prince. It began to speak with a high-pitched squawk. Its eagle-eyebrows creased angrily in a frown. "What on earth are you doing *here* of all places, you foolish child?" it asked. Its breath smelt terrible, like rotten fish.

The young knight nervously told the eagle all about his pilgrimage to Temple.

The creature opened its beak and squawked, laughing. The prince felt sick at the smell of its breath, but he dare not cover his mouth for fear of upsetting it.

"If you want to find the Knights Templar," it said, "you will need to fight a creature called the Bagely Ghost. If you don't kill the Bagely Ghost, you won't find the Knights Templar, and what's more, you will be torn to pieces." The eagle-angel creature stopped to frown again, "very small pieces, boy."

With that statement, the creature stopped talking and it flew off dramatically into the blue sky. It perched upon the tallest cedar tree in the forest, quite some distance away, ruffling its white wings as if to shake dirt away.

The prince squinted his eyes in the ever-brightening sun, and then looked back towards the road.

It felt strange to be having so many frightening experiences on such a bright and beautiful day. He always thought that scary things only happened at night time, or in the cold and dark winter months.

Today was the strangest day of the prince's life.

Chapter Four: The Old Kirk

The prince continued walking down the Old Road, looking back nervously to make sure that the eagle-angel creature wasn't following him.

He felt that he was slowly approaching Temple, but he couldn't explain how he knew this. Perhaps it was the way that the northern mountains became smaller hills. His mother had told him once that this was a sign of reaching the South.

What is more is that the cottages he saw on the edge of the Old Road were a colour he had never seen. His mother had once said that the strange people in the South made their houses out of something called sandstone. "Peasants!" she had once said, "imagine using sandstone instead of granite to build houses! What tramps!"

A voice inside the prince told him to move off the road, to a pathway on the left. As he knew that following his intuition was important in Aberdreams, he did just that. Intuition was like a friend here.

He pushed through a lot of prickly shrubs and found himself in a lush pine forest. He walked through a glen where a beautiful river washed clear water over moss-green rocks. The trickling sound of the water calmed his nerves a little, but he still felt uneasy for some reason.

The prince walked through the glen and found himself within a little cemetery full of gravestones that had strange images of skulls and crossbones.

An ancient stone chapel stood in the centre of the cemetery.

"This is it," he said to himself, "this is Temple!"

Suddenly, he became aware of a little old man sitting on a stone bench. The man was so extremely old that he looked as if he was incapable of moving.

The old man was quietly crying, which moved the prince to reach out to him. He asked the old man what was wrong, and the wee man gave the strangest reply with a voice so weak that it was barely a whisper.

"I can't do the things I need to do, laddie," said the old man. "I can't die and get my eternal rest! The Bagely Ghost won't let me die! He won't let me rest, and I'm ready to go…oh I'm so exhausted, son. I have lived for such a long time….I just want to go. I want to die! Why won't he let me die?"

The Bagely Ghost! Hadn't that horrible eagle creature with the fishy breath told the prince that he needed to kill the Bagely Ghost to become a Templar Knight?

The prince asked him if there was anything that he could do to help. The old man's face lit up. "Yes, son," he wheezed, "I know about your three items from nature. If you use them correctly, you can get rid of the Bagely Ghost for me. And if the Bagely Ghost dies, I will get my rest – and you will become a knight. Now, you know who the Bagely Ghost is, don't you?"

The young prince shook his head. The way the old man asked the question made him feel as if he really *should* have known who the Bagely Ghost was.

"No? Well, laddie, I'm afraid that you are not very sharp. Look here, do you remember that eagle-headed swine you met on the Old Road? That's him. That's the Bagely Ghost!"

The old man wheezed and coughed into his hand, as if the simple act of talking was too much for him.

The prince was shocked. The eagle-angel had been talking about *himself!* The Bagely Ghost was challenging the prince to kill him! Why on earth would he do such a thing?

The old man continued talking, but a little faster and louder than before. "Now, we must be quick. The Bagely Ghost is on his way here now to fight you, and he cannot abide water. You must throw your magic stone into the ground here as hard as you can, as quick as you can. A crater will appear where you throw your stone. Water will fill up the crater shortly afterwards, and you must then drown The Bagely Ghost in there."

The young prince was starting to regret this mission. That creature was terrifying! Could the prince, who had never fought *anybody*, really kill that big man-bird?

The wise old man continued talking in his hoarse voice, "Laddie, do you remember the dark demon who you met back up north, who came out of the oak tree? Well, he has been following you down The Old Road too, and he is also close. You need to kill *him* with your thistle.

The prince's jaw dropped open.

"It will be easy, trust me, son," said the old man. "The eagle-headed one and the demon shadow both hate thistles!"

"Finally," the wee old man whispered, "you must rub the acorn from the old oak tree three times. Rub it with your thumb in front of this ancient chapel. This is all you need to do boy, but let me spell it out again clearly."

The old man paused for a few seconds to wheeze and cough again before finishing his instructions: "If you kill both of these swine who you met on the Old Road, and you then look upon this chapel whilst rubbing the acorn three times, you will be able to embark on an immortal crusade with the Templars."

The prince was silent. He didn't understand why he needed to do such weird things.

"Once the shadow demon and the eagle-headed one are dead, I too will no longer be tormented by them. I will die and find my peace. We will *both* be happy."

The prince was beginning to feel brave. It was now or never.

He threw the stone into the earth with all the force that he could muster. The earth shuddered, the old man nearly fell off his bench, and a crater appeared where the stone had landed. The prince and the old man looked down into it in amazement. A huge hole in the earth!

Within an instant, the blue sky turned grey. Heavy rain poured from the sky, filling the crater with water. It overflowed and spilled onto the green grass of the graveyard. The prince's shoes began to squelch in the mud.

And then, there it was. The eagle-headed one. The Bagely Ghost. He appeared from behind the chapel. It moved towards the young prince slowly, hunched over like a stalking cat. Its eagle's beak looked sharper than ever.

The Bagely Ghost jumped towards the young prince. The prince, however, jumped in the air at the same time and grabbed the Bagely Ghost by the neck. He then turned towards the water-filled crater and threw the ugly eagle creature into the hole. *Splash!*

The Bagely Ghost was splashing about and squawking and getting everyone wet with its soaked wings.

The prince calmly pushed the Bagely Ghost's head underwater with his bare hands. He used all the strength he had, avoiding the bird's beak which was trying to peck at his wrists. Its head kept popping up from under the water as it struggled with the prince's grip, and it was screaming like a baby chick.

Then, the Bagely Ghost died. Just like that. It froze in the water and began to float at the top of the crater, like a sick goldfish.

The young prince couldn't believe how easy it was! But…there was no time to relax.

Suddenly, the dark demon from the oak tree appeared – this time from a little door in a yew tree.

The prince darted forward without delay. He grabbed the thistle from his bag and pricked the dark demon in the throat area. The demon's shadow-like body felt much more solid than he thought it would; just like a human body. To the prince's relief, the shadowy demon melted down into some kind of solid black liquid. It created a black pool on the green earth, like hot tar.

The prince stepped back.

The Bagely Ghost and the Shadow Demon were both dead.

Chapter Five: The Hill

The prince turned to the old man, who now had a big smile upon his face. The man looked so relaxed and happy. He closed his eyes on the stone bench and fell gently to his side. He died there and then, peacefully.

The old man's body crumbled into grey dust. The rain, which was still falling, washed it down into the earth beneath the stone bench. The prince felt strangely happy to watch the old man becoming a part of the earth. It was sad, but he knew that it was what the old man wanted.

Once the old man's ashes has disappeared into the soil, the rain stopped. The clouds cleared and the blue sky of summer returned once again.

The young prince had just one more thing to do.

He took the smooth acorn from his pocket and he rubbed it three times with his thumb – just like the old man told him to. He looked directly at the chapel as he rubbed it. It was cool and soft beneath his thumb.

Out of the acorn's smooth surface grew a sharp little needle which pricked the prince's thumb. He instantly felt exhausted; he laid down on the wet grass and fell into a deep sleep.

When the prince woke up, he was overcome with delight. Oh, the beauty of it! He was on top of a large green hill; *the* hill, he just *knew*, where the Knights Templars' treasure was buried.

"This is the most magical place in Scotland", he said to himself. In his mind, he saw a vision of many knights creating this hill with their bare hands to conceal the treasure. "Yes," he said to himself, "this is the sacred spot, the most sacred spot in all of Scotland! This is where the treasure is buried!"

The young man looked up into the blue sky. To his pure joy, he finally saw them: the Knights Templar. There were hundreds of them, riding through the summer sky on their horses in some kind of parade. They were ghostly and dream-like, as if they themselves were clouds too.

The knight at the front of the parade looked down upon the prince. He began to gallop towards him on his beautiful white horse. The horse pranced through the sky as if it was swimming underwater, slowly and with grace, white as mist. The prince felt quietly ecstatic with the sight of such beauty. He had never smiled that much before in his life; his face hurt from grinning and yet he couldn't stop!

"Now child, it is your turn to be a knight," said the knight on the white horse. "You have defeated the black demon and the Bagely Ghost. You helped the wise old man pass over to the Otherworld. You have found the most sacred spot in Moorfoot, where our treasure is buried. As your reward, you will join us. We will ride the skies. We will save people from their destruction, wherever they need us, and you will become one of us forevermore. Rise up now, and become an immortal knight."

The young knight, without trying, began to float. The air was warm and he felt free, floating upwards towards the knights. He looked down at the hills below, which were getting smaller and smaller, and he didn't feel scared at all. It was fun. He was free!

The prince reached out towards the main knight. The knight took his hand and helped him to settle on the back of his beautiful white horse.

They rode off together in the great procession, slowly becoming a part of the white clouds, blending into them until no knights or horses could be seen – just clouds.

It is said that the young prince can still be seen in the skies of Scotland from time to time, dressed in armour and riding a beautiful white horse of his own.

Look out for the young prince in the skies of Temple. Surely, if he is to be seen at all, it will be in the skies of that sleepy little village which he was once so desperate to find.

&

The witch finishes reading the tale. The pages of the old leather book flitter this way and that way again. The book closes with an angry slam, spitting dust in her face. She coughs.

The witch nods her head. She understands something new. She moves on to her next vision.

※

WISE CROW SPEAKS: The Old Road is an old folktale from Aberdeenshire. In the only remaining version of this story, the prince in the tale is desperate to find the 'land of the Knights Templar'. Although Temple (or Balantrodoch as it was once called) is not explicitly mentioned in the tale, it is quite possible that this was the destination implied by the people who once shared it. Regardless (metaphorically speaking) all Knights Templar roads in Scotland once led back to Temple, making this tale and Temple intrinsically connected.

Christiana's House

WISE CROW SPEAKS: This story was preserved in the writings of the Knights Hospitallers, the order who took over the Knights Templars' Scottish property when the Templars dissolved in 1312. It is likely to have taken place some time in the 1200s.

⁊⁕

Christiana pushes open the door to her beloved home in Esperston, near Balantrodoch. She is frail and old. It has been many years since she has stepped foot in this place, her only true home; the place where her three little boys had once squealed and played and danced. The place where her husband, William (who she refuses to reflect upon in any detail), would sit and eat, slobbering in the rocking chair.

The sitting room is dusty and ice cold. It is grey, dead. This large house is not the place it was. Despite its size and its elegance, it was once so warm, such a home. But the Scottish Knights Templar have turned it into a joyless *property*.

The few things that the Knights Templar have left here have nothing of the warm Christianity that she embraces within her own faith. No images of friendly Saints exuding warmth and compassion. Besides her old furniture, there is little more here than a few unwanted goblets and a stone holy cross statue on a shelf she doesn't recognise. The sitting room is a dark cobwebbed void where happy children once played.

Christiana blows a storm of dust off her old armchair, which starts a coughing frenzy. When she regains her breath, she takes in the chair. It has eroded over the years, but underneath the thick layer of dust, the pale wood is still trying to show itself.

Christiana sits down and begins to weep. She looks at her right hand, at the stump where her little finger used to be. This sight of the stump no longer traumatises her. She no longer feels that she has to hide her hand from everyone's sight (including her own). Far worse has happened to her since she lost her finger.

Her thoughts return to the house, to her history. This was the place where she had lived ever since she was a little girl. She cared nothing for its financial 'value', this was *home,* the place with the garden where she had sat under the apple tree looking for fairies. The place where teenage summers had been spent lying on the grass, watching butterflies pass through the sky, wondering what life would be like when she grew up. On winter nights, she would lie by the sitting room fireplace watching her mother knit and her father stare at the wall paintings in gentle contemplation.

Christiana looks at the old rocking chair where her husband used to sit. She recalls William picking his nose and farting; a disgusting man to conjure directly after the memory of her contemplative father.

Christiana's face tightens. Why did she ever marry William? The wastrel! The lazy, devious swine! He destroyed her life!

No, Christiana, no, she thinks, *we don't reflect upon William. It was a happy home.*

※

William had been desperate to become a Knights Templar, and the order was very willing to welcome him – on the provisor that he signed all of his wife's property over to them. It was technically illegal (Christiana owned everything) but the Knights Templar were powerful – and what the Knights Templar wanted, the Knights Templar got.

※

Christiana fought the Knights Templar hard on the day that they first came banging on her door to claim her house. They came just weeks after William had died, on a day when none of her grown-up sons was at home.

She pushed back against the door as they attempted to force it open, like a tiny squirrel pressing pathetically against a falling tree. *This is OUR property, woman!* the henchmen shouted. *It is NO place for a widow! Get OUT, OUT and give us our rightful property! OUT, WOMAN, OUT!*

She continued to press against the door with her back, putting all of her force against the two men outside, but it was impossible. Feeling herself giving way to the struggle, in a last desperate attempt she turned around and grabbed the slowly-opening door. She didn't really know what she was doing, she was sweating, panicking, she just needed to grab hold of something.

A shock of pain overcame her hand, like the whole thing had been forced into a sink of ice-cold water. She screamed. Her vision became a sea of black followed by an explosion of electric patterns. The pain moved up her arm into her shoulder.

One of the henchmen had sliced her little finger clean off with a dagger, just below the knuckle. It bounced off the doorstep like a piece of rubber.

Christiana fell to the floor. Whilst she was unconscious, a henchman rolled her onto the lawn, like an old rug for relocation.

ॐ

In the late 13th Century, Brian de Jay was the head of the Scottish Knights Templar. It was under his command that Christiana's property was ordered to be stolen. Christiana did successfully manage to regain control of her land by petitioning the King. However, Brian de Jay was determined. He later managed to evict her *again* when the area became destabilised by wars between Scotland and England.

Christiana spent much of her life battling the Templars for her home. She was not proud – she simply wanted to live in peace in the place where she had grown. She was attached to the place, especially the sitting room where her peaceful mother and father had sat together in quiet love.

Christiana was forced to live in a tiny hut on the side of the estate – the only part of the property which Brian de Jay and the Templars had 'allowed' her to keep. Her main company was in the form of regular visits from her beloved sons.

The only other close human contact that Christiana encountered was with a young local woman, Meg, who she would see in the local woodlands. Christiana welcomed their light discussions about the seasons and the fascinating workings of nature. Meg would listen to her pain and welcome it; a *wise woman of the woods* in the making.

ॐ

It was 1298. Longing to return to her home for her middle years, Christiana asked her beloved son, Richard, to appeal to the Knights Templars directly. He was a charming boy, and the Templars riches were immense. They had outposts and property all over Scotland. What did they even *need* Christiana's home for?

Richard agreed to help her.

Brian de Jay himself was back in Balantrodoch from his travels, but just for a short time. He had brought back a small

SUMMER: Temple and Esperston

troop of Welsh soldiers who were in Scotland to help the English in the Scottish-English war. (Brian de Jay was English and committed to his home country.)

Richard knew that Brian de Jay was in the chapel at Balantrodoch, and so he took his chance.

Arriving via the woodland track to the old chapel was a terrifying experience for Richard. He was a bold young man but he wasn't stupid; he knew the danger that he was in.

Richard stood outside the walls of the chapel, leaning against the cool sandstone. He could hear the sound of swords and armour clanging; men play-fighting like boisterous children in preparation for war. This was the worst possible time for him to make such a request. But here he was.

He heard men speaking a strange language he had never heard, which he guessed to be Welsh. Every now and then he would overhear a phrase in his own language, mingling with foreign words, usually something about the 'savage' or 'uncivilised' Scots.

Richard stood shivering just beyond their reach, behind the wall, unarmed and incapable of defence. He considered running back home, but he imagined the disappointed face of his mother; his kind, warm mother who had lost her finger (and her sanity) to this nonsense. The Knights Templar had barely even stepped foot into her house, his childhood home!

No, he had to go inside. This was his only chance. Brian de Jay was a powerful man, and he would not be in Balantrodoch again any time soon.

Richard took a deep breath. He pushed himself off the safe wall, turned around, and opened the squeaky gate to the chapel. *Of course*, he thought to himself, *squeaky gates*. Twenty or thirty men in armour turned instantly to look at this sheepish young civilian. And just beyond them, standing at the extravagant entrance to the chapel, there he was – Brian de Jay.

ꝏ

Christiana burst into tears. Dust was getting in her eyes and up her nose. She snivelled and sneezed as the tears fell.

What a wretched thing it was to cry in a cloud of dust. Every time she wiped her wet eyes, she would push tiny particles of dust into them, bits of dead Knights Templar skin. Her eyes were itchy and swollen, and despite the warm summer's day outdoors, it was freezing in here, hollow. This was not the home she had been evicted from.

Christiana recalled the day the news came to her, the day that the spotty teenage boy from over the hill came to tell her what had happened to Richard. The boy had been friendly with one of the Welsh soldiers and shared the full story with her.

Brian de Jay had been far more reasonable than Richard had expected. He agreed to hand back the property to Christiana without much persuasion at all. He didn't have any use for it anyway, he said. But, perhaps in return, Richard could do one little favour for him? Would Richard – being a local Scot and knowing the land so well – please be so kind as to lead Brian de

Jay and his troops through the woods, all the way to their English camp in Liston (present-day Kirkliston, Edinburgh)?

Of course, Richard must have known that something wasn't right with this whole story, but he had little option but to accept and hope that the deal was legit.

It wasn't.

When the troops reached Clerkington Woods just a few miles down the road, the captain of the Welsh troops suddenly turned on Richard and butchered him to death. His mutilated remains were left at the trunk of a young hawthorn tree. The troops spat on his remains and marched on to Liston. They knew quite well how to get there.

&

Christiana spent the final years of her life mostly drowning in guilt and whisky. Her home, which she had coveted so badly, had become a place of torment. It was a pointless cage which her son had died for. Why couldn't she have been happy in the little hut? Why couldn't she have just let it go?

Christiana's life wasn't all misery in those final years, however. In her old age, she would take to walking through Clerkington Woods, where Richard had died. She wandered slow and grey like a rain cloud. On long summer days, she would stay there for hours, walking over little wooded hills and pushing herself through scratchy juniper tree pathways. She would breathe in the warm air and pluck fresh blueberries.

Once, she saw her old friend Meg, who looked almost as old and grey as Christiana, yet still with that youthful spark still in her eyes. Meg took Christiana into her arms and let her cry until she was dry.

Christiana could feel Richard's presence everywhere in those woods. He was in the soil, and so she would walk barefoot on it, kissing the cool earth with her feet. Richard was a part of these woods in the same way that a falling leaf is a part of the soil or like a wave is a part of the ocean.

Christiana would imagine little people living under the hills in the woods. She didn't know why, but it soothed her to think of faeries or elves living under there. She remembered searching for faeries as a little girl. She started to do the same again in these woods.

She would often stop at a little withered hawthorn tree and feel a strange emotion, as if tiny fleas were crawling all over her body. Itchy, uncomfortable, urgent. It was a fearful sensation, like death was upon her skin, and yet she felt compelled to stay there for long periods. She would rest against the bendy trunk and peep at the sun through its branches. Over time, the uncomfortable feeling subsided and she grew to love it there more than anywhere else in the woods.

The poor hawthorn was hanging on for life, just like she was.

Christiana talked to the tree often. Richard was a part of the bark. He would hear her every word.

She would feel the dryness of the spiky branches brush against her neck, and felt that Richard was reaching out to comfort her.

When it rained – which it often did in Lowland summer evenings – she wouldn't seek shelter under larger trees. She stayed under the hawthorn and got drenched. She would let the water fall onto the leaves of the tree, and then drip down onto her. As her skin absorbed the raindrops, Christiana became more than one person, just like she had been all those years ago when she would stroke her pregnant belly with pride.

When her time came, Christiana laid down in the rain and died at the trunk of the old hawthorn tree. As she breathed her final breath, she smiled.

❧

WISE CROW SPEAKS: The woodlands where Richard was murdered is now home to Rosebery Reservoir – a human-made loch that rests quietly within little green knowes. This beautiful place has an eerie stillness that persists even during stormy weather.

AUTUMN:

Borthwick and Gladhouse

Saint Mungo and The Cross

WISE CROW SPEAKS: In Scottish legend, Saint Mungo was the grandchild of King Lot, whose ancient fortification sat upon Traprain Law in East Lothian. It is suspected that the word 'Lothian' came from King Lot, who famously threw his daughter, Princess Thenew, from the top of Traprain Law as punishment for her 'illegitimate' pregnancy.

By divine intervention, Princess Thenew and her unborn child survived. She sailed over to Fife and gave birth to a baby boy, Kentigern, who grew up to become the legendary Saint Mungo, Patron Saint of Glasgow.

Saint Mungo spent a reported eight years in Borthwick, a mere 20 miles away from the place where his mother was thrown from the hill by King Lot. Much is known about Saint Mungo's legendary life, and yet his miracle at Borthwick remains practically unknown.

&

It happened sometime in the sixth century.

The community of Borthwick gathered upon a sloping hill that overlooked the old forest. They were there for Saint Mungo, their leader, who stood at the peak of the grassy slope.

It was early morning, and the late September gales were fierce. Dirty grey clouds refused to let an ounce of sunshine beam onto the hills. The first loose leaves of autumn were spinning, cyclone-like, all around the still Saint.

It was a compelling but disconcerting sight. His adoring community kept their distance.

Saint Mungo's brown robes were blown about in all directions by the gales. His straggly brown hair was thrown up and down, left and right, this way, that way, obscuring his face. His body was as stiff as a corpse as his loose garments tried to break free from the rags. Even his wirey beard seemed to be moved by the gales.

I know that you have been struggling, my friends! shouted the Saint. He now held his hair up in a scrunch so that he could see the gathering crowd. At last, his handsome face became visible through his hair, expressing that famous kindness. Thirty or forty people of all ages watched with wide eyes.

I know life is hard here. I know that you do not have enough food, he continued. The crowd made enthusiastic squeals of agreement. *You have lost loved ones to hunger and disease. I have seen the devil of insanity grip you. You feel mad, as if your minds are no longer you own, but no more!*

Hail, Saint Mungo! shouted a toothless woman at the front of the crowd.

The crowd all repeated her cry. *Hail, Saint Mungo!*

There was a confused moment as two of the strongest men in the community made their way up the slope, appearing seemingly out of nowhere. Whatever Saint Mungo had planned for today had clearly been arranged in advance.

AUTUMN: Borthwick and Gladhouse

Saint Mungo looked relieved as he noticed the men dragging two large wooden carts up the hill behind them. Both carts were full of yellow sea sand. When the men reached the Saint, they attached the breaks to the rickety carts and left one cart on each side of the Saint.

The gales continued to howl, and for a moment the Saint had to pinch up his hair with both hands.

Thank you, boys, he mouthed effeminately to the strong men. It was casual, as if they had just handed him a vessel of water.

Today, I will perform a miracle! he shouted over the winds, regaining his masculinity. *I will cure you of your sicknesses!* Fresh green and yellow leaves whirled up and danced around him as if to create a protective circle.

The crowd began an orderly cheer – HAIL SAINT MUNGO! HAIL SAINT MUNGO! A local hunchback man fainted into his wife's strong arms. *Oh, it's too much fae him!* she cried.

Hush now, hush, my children, Saint Mungo asked, ignoring the hunchback and his dramatic wife. He stretched his arms out before him and with flat palms faced down he gestured gently to the earth, as if to lower the energy. *Hush, I will need total silence for this, my friends.*

That is when the miracle took place.

A look of deep concentration took over his face. His thick eyebrows creased, his eyes tightly closed. His face wrinkled inwards like a raisin.

He mumbled something to himself, a kind of mantra, over and over. It was barely audible, but those at the front of the crowd could just about decipher it over the gales. *I reflect, my Lord, on your miraculous resurrection. I reflect, my Lord, on your miraculous resurrection. I reflect, my Lord, on your miraculous resurrection....I reflect, my Lord....*

He slowly raised his arms higher, palms still faced down, as if controlling a string puppet.

Sand began to move out of the wooden carts. It seemed to be attracted to his hands, as if the sand were some kind of metal dust being pulled towards two large magnets.

Underneath his palms, the grains gathered. Saint Mungo began to shape the sand mid-air like a master potter. It was malleable like putty, unconcerned by the gales.

The sand moved from the carts towards Mungo's hands faster and faster. It was a funnel movement, thin at the carts and then congealing beneath his palms. He was shaping the congealing grains so quickly that the sculpture he was creating could not be understood until it was all over. He was calm and in complete control of the process.

The crowd looked on. Shock and awe. Total silence. It seemed to be over as soon as it began. Seconds, perhaps.

Saint Mungo had created a perfect Holy Cross, as tall as the man himself, out of nothing but dry sand.

Come now, come forth children, he smiled, once again pulling his hair back from his eyes. The Holy Cross just stood there on the hill, yellow and impossible in the growing storm.

Each member of the crowd was invited up to touch the cross, one by one. When they touched it (usually with apprehension), Saint Mungo placed his right hand upon their heads and silently blessed them. Each person was then sent away and told to rest at home. *Go home and rest, child,* he would nod and whisper.

It was true that before that day, many people in the community had become severely mentally unwell. The extreme poverty was too much to bear. Breakdowns and suicides were rife. The work of the Devil was strong.

Although it took a while for things to improve in Borthwick, a remarkable thing happened after that day; community mental health improved dramatically. In most cases it happened overnight. The people in the village still dealt with immense hardships, yet it was always with remarkable equanimity.

Word spread. People came from miles around to touch the miraculous Holy Cross. Everyone wanted to receive the blessings of Saint Mungo. By all accounts, the miraculous Holy Cross at Borthwick was the original anti-depressant.

Saint Mungo went on to become one of the most celebrated figures in Scottish myth and legend. Tales of his miracles have survived centuries, such as the time his tears of compassion brought a dead robin back to life. The Saint adored nature, and so it is no surprise that his offering for Borthwick's community was created out of a pure natural substance: sand. In this respect, the Saint promoted nature-connection as a form of healing. *Touch the sand of the Earth and heal, my friends.*

If you ever visit Borthwick, study the soil closely. You may notice a tiny grain or two of sand. Take it home with you. You may be holding a tiny miracle in your hand, and who knows when you might need it?

The Spirits of Borthwick

Part One: Samhain

It is Samhain. Halloween. Winter is stepping forward, but it is not quite here. The veil between the worlds is thin, and Borthwick is coming alive with the spirits of the Otherworld.

The spirits rise each year. Their haunting throughout Samhain is as certain as the yellow maple leaves that fall into Middleton South Burn here.

Borthwick Castle holds many secrets. Most of them are bizarre. At the edge of North Middleton – the largest village in Moorfoot – its twin towers and embattled wall have been dominating the valley below for more than 600 years.

To the unknowing eye, one of its towers looks in disrepair, as if rotting away near the top windows. This (otherwise beautifully preserved) fortification is, however, simply showing its history; this damage is from a cannon scar left by Oliver Cromwell's army in 1650.

The deciduous trees of autumn complement the stone masonry of Borthwick Castle perfectly. Amongst its cream pastel stone exterior are numerous orange and brown bricks, dotted about at random like an autumnal Lego experiment.

From the castle's entrance, a view of the jagged Pentland Hills dominates the distant skyline. Closer, soft valley hills hide the (deceptively close) neighbouring village of North Middleton.

Currie Wood, to the south of the castle, feels alive with the wee folk – faeries – whose presence can be felt throughout the hilly woodland paths. These paths lead southward towards Currie Inn, where ancient locals who worshipped the legendary Faery Stane buried their loved ones.

※

Next to the castle sits a smaller – but no less intriguing – partner building; Borthwick Parish Church. With an original structure dating back to the 12th century, this gothic building nests within a wild overgrown graveyard.

Gnarled yew trees, whose red berries are as pretty as they are poisonous, guard the church. Stone carvings of grotesque, deformed little faces poke out from the side of the church's exterior, taunting visitors.

Mossy walls crumble away at the south of the church. Middleton South Burn trickles over fallen trees and million-year-old rocks here. Wonky gravestones listen to the sound of the burn washing the earth clean.

It is here, down by the burn, where a woman's spirit sits today. This spirit knows herself to be Margaret Unes. She has remembered her 17th century life in Borthwick. She has remembered the witchcraft accusations. She recalls being strangled and burned in the nearby town of Dalkeith; a town that enjoyed strangling and burning women more than most. She gently touches her neck, looking for proof.

Margaret has travelled throughout Moorfoot, exploring its myths and its stories, and she is almost at the end of her journey. Before she takes her final steps, she has come to this spot to join the yearly Samhain Spirits of Borthwick. Together, they will mourn the horrors of years gone by.

It is daytime. The sky is crisp blue. Margaret sits by the burn and looks up the slope, which is carpeted with so many yellow and brown leaves that no earth is visible. She eyes the sharp spire of Borthwick Church: a crucifix. It looks like a weapon to her.

She looks further ahead towards the castle and notices a mass of wild ferns in the earth, still green with summer's goodness. A tall copse of maple trees almost hides the towers of the castle, yet she is a barely a stones throw away from it.

Here, by the burn, she is as low down as you could possibly be in Borthwick.

Margaret feels stirrings in Currie Wood. The spirits are arriving. She doesn't see anything significant, or hear anything distinct, or smell anything strong; each of her senses pick up tiny changes in unison, creating the unmistakable feeling of arrival. Barely audible whispers in the woods accompany vague shadows in the corner of her eye.

Startled, Margaret hears three loud knocks coming from within the church. She turns toward the spirit of the old minister William Traill, who appears in the graveyard, a shadow congealing into human shape. The black and white colours of religious robes and a wrinkled peachy face materialise. He looks up at the roof crucifix which is boasting against the blue of the sky.

Margaret hugs herself in fear, like a lost little girl. However, not for the first time recently, she marvels at how she simply *knows* what is happening. The names of people she has never met before are clear to her, like William Traill, and their life stories seem to be a part of her natural memory bank.

ॐ

William Traill was Borthwick's minister for quite some time in the late 17th century. Whilst he lived here, he would often wake up in the night, at around 3am, to the sound of three mysterious knocks on his bedroom door. This would often happen the night before he was due to offer an important sermon. If William ignored the knocks and tried to rest, three more knocks would come – this time on his bedhead. The bedhead knocks stopped after a few occasions – but only because he would always get out of bed after the door knocks! For William, the knocks were a sign that he needed to plan his sermons, and so he would simply get out of bed and begin working. At times he was grateful for the encouragement.

AUTUMN: Borthwick and Gladhouse

William became less frightened by the knocks as time went by. When he later turned old and frail, the knocks ceased. He died in 1714, leaving three sons who all become ministers in his footsteps.

ॐ

Margaret looks ahead through the maple trees, towards the towers of Borthwick Castle. What she sees now is not so much a ghost of a *person*, but rather the ghost of an *incident*; a moment in time so remarkable that the landscape has captured it.

A young man runs down the slope from the road above. He hops over the stream next to Margaret (oblivious to her), panting in a frenzy, and disappears into Currie Wood.

Margaret smiles, knowing that that this 'boy' is in fact Mary Queen of Scots.

Mary lived at Borthwick Castle for a stint in 1567. She famously escaped a siege attempt by butching up as a page boy and escaping down a rope through one of the castle's narrow windows.

ॐ

Stalking the embattled wall now is a muddy young woman in medieval garb. Ann Grant was a live-in servant in Borthwick Castle who haunts the 'red chamber' room. Her hauntings have been felt so strongly by visitors that the castle's owners once ordered an exorcism.

Hundreds of years ago, the lord of the castle, who was having extra-marital relations with Ann, found out that she was pregnant with his child. He swiftly had her executed, by sword no less, in the red chamber room, to avoid having her claim any rights to the castle. Visions of her murder scene have flashed before more than one person in the red room. One visitor recalled seeing Ann being slashed across the stomach by a soldier, whilst two maids pinned her down on the bed.

Scratching sounds have been heard in the red room many times.

Inexplicable scratch-like marks reappear even after fresh paint jobs.

Footsteps are heard when nobody is around.

Doors slam on fingers and toes. (Men are usually the victims.)

The cries of Ann are joined by the unintelligible rantings of a facially disfigured man. This man's skin appears to have been burned so badly that it has half-melted away, like cheese that has bubbled prior to crisping. This spirit is the shadow of an in-house chancellor who was burned alive by the castle's owners following accusations of embezzlement.

❧

The final sight is one that Margaret is the most disturbed by: the sight of a man about to jump from one tower to another. He hesitates and seems to be judging the distance, indicating that at any moment he will take the leap.

Prisoners in the old parish of Borthwick were offered freedom if they were able to make the (11 foot) jump from one tower to another. Margaret remembers these stories from her past life and looks away in horror. She hears the man fall to the ground; his body thumps like a sack of rock. She understands that this grotesque game was a simple pleasure for the rich. They abused the poor here as casually as they hunted rabbits. She feels a quiet anger rising.

The pain and the sorrow all around her becomes too much.

Fury rises.

She stands up and lets out an almighty scream in solidarity with her fellow spirits. Her body bends forward, her blonde hair flies wildly and her wide open mouth seems big enough to suck in the whole of Borthwick.

The spirits turn away from their misery to watch Margaret, who is, after all, simply another one of them.

The scream lasts forever. A universe escapes from her.

Slowly, eventually, she is exhausted. She stops. She looks down to the grass. There is nothing left.

Dusk falls.

Spirits fade, and shadows move back through Currie Wood.

One spirit, however, remains.

Down by the river, Margaret Unes replays what happened to her here in Borthwick, back in 1628. It is all very clear to her now.

Part Two: WISE CROW SPEAKS

For hundreds of years, the Lowlands of Scotland were a very dangerous place to be a woman. Accusations of witchcraft were rife, and 'guilty' people were executed by hanging at the stake. Their bodies were immediately burned where they hung.

Some of the executed people (mostly women) *may* have been involved in alternative spiritual practices not condoned by the Christian majority. However, this would have been in a relatively small number of cases. Even then, it often amounted to little more than the concoction of herbal remedies – these people were healers. This is particularly unjust if we consider that many of these women were simply trying to help their communities who may have had no other medicine available to them.

All it took was for something to go wrong, for example for someone to get sick after an administration of a herbal remedy, and a woman could be accused of murder by the means of witchcraft.

Most people, however, were accused of witchcraft simply because someone in the community didn't like them. Such an accusation was a great tool for enacting revenge on your nemesis.

The most executions for witchcraft in Scotland happened within the Lothians. Executions in the Lothians were double that of the Strathclyde region (including Glasgow, which later became Scotland's largest city) and they were way more rife than in every other region of Scotland. This was at a time when the population of Scotland was far more fairly spread across the country than it is these days.

According to *The Survey of Scottish Witchcraft**, 32% of the (up to four thousand) accused witches came from the Lothians, compared to 14% from the Strathclyde area. 12% were from Fife, 9% were from the Scottish Borders and 7% were from Grampian. The numbers continue to decrease in all other areas.

In short, the Lothians were rampant with witch-fear.

What is interesting about the accusations of witchcraft in the old Parish of Borthwick is that exactly one-third of the accused were men (six out of 18 recorded cases).

What brought about such large-scale persecutions of men in the area (33% compared to 15% of male accusations in Scotland as a whole) is not known. We do, however, know about one who got away!

George Simbeard was accused of witchcraft some 21 years after Margaret Unes was executed. In desperation, he claimed mistaken identity to the authorities. Luckily for him, the authorities believed him long enough for him to disappear into the sunset. By the time they realised that he *was* indeed the George Simbeard who they were after, it was too late. George was gone. Hopefully he went on to lead a peaceful and happy life somewhere away from persecution.

AUTUMN: *Borthwick and Gladhouse*

We don't know much about Margaret Unes herself, but what we do know is very interesting:

Margaret Unes was accused of witchcraft in her home Parish of Borthwick in 1628.

She confessed to having a pact with the Devil and also to renouncing her baptism. (It is worth noting that torture and sleep deprivation were often used as methods to extract 'confessions' from people.)

She was accused of murdering – through supernatural means – the Earl of Lothian.

She was accused of using witchcraft to kill Lord Borthwick plus his wife and children.

Margaret was reportedly in league with another witch from Edinburgh, Janet Schitlingtoun (who we know even less about). They were both sent to court in Dalkeith, a large Midlothian town south of Edinburgh where witch trials were common.

Margaret Unes and Janet Schitlingtoun stood trial in 1628, and that is the last we ever heard of them. It is safe to assume that they were both executed.

One final piece of information we know about Margaret Unes is this:

She liked to be called Meg by her friends.

ɞ

All of the spirits that Margaret sees in this story represent bonafide myths and legends surrounding the area of Borthwick.

ɞ

*Goodare, Martin, Miller and Yeoman, 'The Survey of Scottish Witchcraft', http://www.shca.ed.ac.uk/witches/, archived January 2003, accessed 20 August 2021

The Witch, The Lost Girl, and The Willow Stick

Part One: The Lost Girl

The ragged girl has been lost for days. She is hungry. Wet. Freezing. She is exhausted from crying hard tears for her Mam. How did she get so lost? Is she going to die? What are all those strange noises that she keeps hearing here at the loch? What scary monsters live on those big green hills over there? Will they come to get her when she sleeps in the bushes tonight?

Her Mam had told her not to wander off. Not to walk into the woods at the bottom of the village. She got carried away with her imagination, talking to the fairies, and before she knew it she was lost, panicking, crying, falling over on muddy pathways and getting scraped by prickly junipers.

Autumn sits on the cusp of winter. The geese fly in their thousands above, honking as if laughing at her stupidity.

She has been sleeping in the woods for the last two nights, shivering and crying. She spends her days walking on and on, seemingly in circles. *Where's Temple gan? Where's ma Mam? Am a gonnae be found deid in the pathway? Why is there naebody around, no one person? Jesus please help me an ah'll stop talkin tae the fairies like ah promised ma Mam! Why do these paths never end, an never lead anywhere except…..*

The big loch. She had heard people call it a 'reservoir'. People in the village still called it 'new', but they had been talking about it for her whole life and she is nearly eight years old, so it couldn't be *that* new.

She realises now just how far away from Temple she is. She sees the sign by the water: *Gladhouse Reservoir*. She sits at the edge of the water, shivering, drinking cold water with icy hands.

Next, she is watching birds of all kinds – ducks, geese, an oystercatcher – flying from the loch's shores to a little island in the middle of the water and back again. The island is reflected perfectly in the still water, blending with its shadow, making it look like a big round ball.

As she watches the island, something happens to her. Something changes. She feels calm, at peace. The anxiety stops completely. It is as if the stillness of the water seeped within her when she drank it, cooling her blood and her body. She feels as calm and as still as the small trees growing upon the pretty little island.

Am gonnae die, she thinks. And she smiles. *Am gonnae die the night, and I dinnae mind. Am ready tae go noo.*

She feels joyous. Ice cold, numb, and joyous.

She is watching red and brown leaves float slowly upon the water in front of her. She realises that it doesn't matter. She is so happy to just let go of the worry! This water, it is in her body. This body, it will rest in the soil. The geese might eat a bit of her in the soil, and she will become part of the geese. She will fly across the sky, honking and looking down on Temple, the wee village where she had once lived as a silly girl who strayed too far away from her Mam. A silly wee girl who broke her Mam's heart by dying at the big loch that the clever men built down by the hills.

Part Two: Meg and the Willow Stick

Meg is coming back to Blackhope Scar. Almost a year has passed since Thomas The Rhymer shared the Prophecy of Destruction with her and handed her the Willow Stick.

This is the land where you died, maiden, the voice had said to her, *and one day, much of it will be underwater. This whole land is called Moorfoot now, not just the settlement below. You can be the one to destroy it all, maiden – if you choose.*

She looks down at the Willow Stick in her hand. She has kept the Willow Stick with her for the whole year, through all of the seasons, right up until this point where autumn is turning once again into grim winter. It has shown her the lost myths of Moorfoot. It was her reason for returning to life.

Time is a strange thing here. It is many years at the same time for Meg. It is the past and the present. (This type of thing can happen on the cusp of winter – especially for the dead.)

Meg *could* throw the stick against the hill and set the Prophecy in motion, like the voice that came with Thomas The Rhymer had suggested. She *could* watch the hill burst with water, watch it explode, and watch Moorfoot drown.

But Meg she has no intention of doing that, and she never has.

AUTUMN: Borthwick and Gladhouse

She approaches Gladhouse Reservoir, aware that she is not quite in the right time zone. She leans over the rocky shore and gently places the willow stick upon the still water. She watches it slowly twist around on the surface of the water like the spokes of an old wheel; not floating away from her, just calmly turning in one spot.

She can see through the clear water to the bottom of the reservoir. It is shallow, and a shoal of tiny fish dash past looking for a safe place to shelter.

Meg is aware of a small girl's body resting on the bank, just to her right. The girl's breath is shallow. Meg leans towards her. *Ah'm here for ye, little yen*, she whispers.

The lost girl is Meg's final calling before she climbs Blackhope Scar.

Prior to finding herself at the reservoir, Meg had been moving through a muddy pathway. She had been deliberately walking within sight of a sweat-dripping stocky man in a Police uniform, leading him this way for a mile or so. Meg's glass-sharp intuition knew that something important would happen here before she rests up in the hills again. Something healing, right here at the loch. Whenever the Policeman would lose sight of her, she would allow herself to slowly appear before him again, leading him back in the direction of the loch.

You there, lassie! Can ya no hear me? Have you seen a wean, a wee girl? Stop! Lassie! I demand you stop, the noo! Stop, the noo!

When the police officer finally reaches the loch, he looks right through Meg and darts for the little girl lying there on the bank.

As the little girl is about to give up – to close her eyes on the bank of the cold loch and just let go – she hears his voice in a distant bubble.

Elsie! Stay where y'are hen, y'alright! It's me, Constable Oliver from Temple! Am here tae take ya hame, lassie!

The man whips up the half-dead little girl into his arms. Meg is invisible to him. The little girl flops like a bloody rag doll in his arms. She wakes up, moaning, delirious, her brown hair tangled, her skin covered in scratches and muck, her tattered dress little more than a filthy dishcloth.

The girl will live.

Meg turns away from them both. She smiles, satisfied. She turns away from the floating Willow Stick, which has now started to float off towards the little island.

The Prophecy of Destruction can find its own way into the world. Meg needn't be its facilitator.

Meg Unes climbs Blackhope Scar, back to where she woke last winter. So many ages and eras have passed within the last year, and she is sleepy.

The geese fly above Meg. A huge diagonal skein, like a manic chevron, sings *we are home, we are home,* as the 'witch' – the woman – climbs up and up and up.

Hail begins to pelt. It pelts through Meg's body as she reaches the top of the windswept hill. She glances to her side at a small ancient stone building that she hadn't noticed last time, and gets a mental flash of a monk living there many years ago.

But the image dies before it develops any further. She has let go of the Willow Stick now. She has let go of the visions, the myths. The monk vision is just a hangover from its power.

Sheer exhaustion is felt, even in spirit bones. Meg needs her forever rest.

She finds the spot, the place where she woke up last year. Brown grass, sludge. That incredible view over the hilly Lowlands of Scotland.

She takes off her brown robe and lets it drop to her side.

She lies naked on the earth, entering its womb.

The grim skies spit even more fierce hailstone upon her, turning autumn into winter in that very moment. Her blonde hair mingles with the brown earth.

And then, she hears the sound of music, the strings of the harp.

The myths of Moorfoot flash before her one last time.

First, it is sight of the Faery Stane, that majestic rocky globe upon Cowbrae Hill. The sun is behind it, casting shade upon Meg's vision.

Next, a white light sphere flashes against black night sky.

A stick breaks away from an old oak tree.

A hare runs into a cottage.

An angry kilted man chases boys with a sword.

A knight in armour rides a horse against a blue sky.

A frail old woman hugs a withered hawthorn tree.

A sandy holy cross appears, and then….

She sees her final images.

The towers of Borthwick Castle.

The Spirits of Samhain.

Her old life.

Her terrifying death.

Her mother, Marion.

Yes, oh! My mam was called Marion!

Mam!

Come here ma wee darlin' says a big warm lady.

Meg leans forward and lets go of everything, crying with joy as she falls safely into her mother's arms.

The sweet music of the harp lulls Meg as she fades away.

Rest, wee lassie, says the gruff voice of Thomas The Rhymer.

For the second time, Meg Unes slips away from this world.

For the first time, she goes peacefully.

ൠ

WISE CROW SPEAKS (one last time): In 1903, a report from a local newspaper reported that Constable Oliver from Temple Police Station (now somebody's home) had found a little girl wandering about near Gladhouse Reservoir. Apparently she was "in a distressed state" and had been missing for several days.

It was a small story, in a small newspaper, about a small girl who wandered from her small village. Not very remarkable in the grand scheme of things, perhaps. But such an experience – to be a lost vulnerable child amongst lochs and hills for days – surely would have no small impact upon a person's life. The Lost Girl's story honours the countless unknown human stories that are never captured in print or shared; lives lived and forgotten, in terror and in joy.

It is here that our visions end, with a small girl returning to her Mam (hopefully to a happy and loving life) whilst the spirit of a wronged woman finds peace at last.

꿍

A Spell for Meg Unes

Meg (we hope that it is okay to call you Meg), we hope that being brought back to life in these pages has honoured you. We know that in times past there existed two types of witches in Scotland: the fabulous supernatural hags of folklore, and people like you; just normal human beings who were done a terrible injustice.

We blow out the candle now, and with the smoke we send our compassion and respect out for you, and others like you. We send it over the hills and lochs of Scotland. Feel it! The smoke is travelling, going, going, going on beyond, and it will keep on going on beyond, always becoming. *Yes! Out it goes, across Europe, across the whole world, reaching everyone who needs it.*

We honour you, Meg. We honour you all.

Since this book was written, I have discovered a fascinating historical event from Moorfoot which relates directly to Meg Unes.
For more information, scan below.

https://naturetherapyonline.net/moorfoot-blog/hirendean

Old Moorfoot

Above image: The grand opening of Gladhouse Reservoir (formerly known as Moorfoot Loch) in 1879. The Moorfoot Hills can be seen across the water. For the Lost Girl of 1903, the area would have looked much like this. Today, it is surrounded by small pine woodlands and a wetland area; it has become a roosting and nesting site for many bird species. (Image taken from *Illustrated London News* 1879, artist unknown.)

Left: A photo of Temple Village, sometime around 1900–1910. A woman, surrounded by children, collects water from the village well. The wee boy on the far left (smoking a pipe) is thought to be Jock Gilchrist, the boy who Bertram chased with a sabre. (Photographer unknown.)

Acknowledgements

Many thanks to the following people who made this book possible:

All at the Scottish Storytelling Centre for so much support, inspiration and funding. Andy Hunter for leaving a legacy that helped to create this book. Daniel Allison, Janis MacKay, Linda Williamson and David Campbell for the mentoring and advice. Chris McCabe for encouraging me to write. Sarah Crewe for the eagle-eye proofreading. Lily LeMaire for the incredible artwork. Bill Brown for introducing me to Bertram and for the Templars lore. John Kerry for sharing Christiana's story with me. Matthew Vogan for the Borthwick lore. Betty Quinn for offering advice that led me to the St. Mungo story. Drew Kirk for his insightful phone call. Allison Galbraith and Lea Taylor for the helpful emails. Dalkeith Public Library for the enchanting local interest books. The School of Scottish

Studies and Tobar an Dualchais/Kist o Riches for the support and the old recordings. And (as always) my partner Łukasz Waclawski for so much encouragement and support.

Bibliography

Anderson, Alastair, *The 1987 Yearbook of the Gorebridge and District Local History Society* (Gorebridge Yesterdays, 1987)

Chambers, Robert, *Popular Rhymes of Scotland* (W & R Chambers Limited, Edinburgh and London, 1841)

Clunie, John, *Statistical Accounts of Scotland: Borthwick, County of Edinburgh, OSA, Vol. XIII* (William Creech, 1794)

Coventry, Martin, *Haunted Castles and Houses of Scotland*, (Goblinshead, 2004)

Douglas, David, *The Mid-Lothian Esks and their Associations from the Source to the Sea* (David Douglas self-publication, 1895)

Fairgrieve, George, *The 1983 Yearbook of the Gorebridge and District Local History Society* (Gorebridge Yesterdays, 1983)

Fee, McHardy and Smith, *Edinburgh Old Town: Journeys and Evocations* (Luath Press, 2014)

Ferguson, Robert, *The Knights Templar and Scotland* (The History Press, 2010)

Fraser, Andrew, *Brief Notes Compiled for the Midlothian School Trek Camps* (Midlothian Education Committee, 1954)

Galbraith and Willis, *Dancing with Trees*, The History Press, 2017)

Hennessey, Andrew, *Alien Encounters and the Paranormal: The Scottish Experience* (CreateSpace Independent Publishing Platform, 2015)

Levack, Brian P, *Witchcraft in Scotland* (Garland Publishing Inc, 1992)

Mackenzie, Donald A, *Wonder Tales from Scottish Myth and Legend* (Frederick A. Stokes, 1917)

Mackinlay, James, *Folklore of Scottish Lochs and Springs* (William Hodge & Co, 1893)

McCue, Peter, *Britain's Paranormal Forests: Encounters in the Woods* (The History Press, 2019)

Unknown Author, *Temple Old Kirk, A Brief History* (Temple Old Kirk Friends, 2021)

Westwood and Kingshill, *The Lore of Scotland,* Arrow Books, 2009)

Wright, Thomas, *Statistical Accounts of Scotland: Borthwick, County of Edinburgh, NSA, Vol 1* (Blackwoods and Sons 1845)

Online Resources

Carson, Ann, 'Borthwick Castle', Borthwicks of Scotland, Australia, New Zealand & Philadelphia USA, http://freepages.rootsweb.com/~anncarson/genealogy/Borthwick/borthwickcastle.htm, accessed 10 June 2021

Goodare, Martin, Miller and Yeoman, 'The Survey of Scottish Witchcraft', http://www.shca.ed.ac.uk/witches/, archived January 2003, accessed 20 August 2021

James R.E, Captain, 'Midlothian Ordnance Survey Name Books: Volume 56 (OS1/11/56/11)', https://scotlandsplaces.gov.uk/digital-volumes/ordnance-survey-name-books/midlothian-os-name-books-1852-1853/midlothian-volume-56/11, accessed 5 June 2021

Lauri, Dr, 'Mysteries of the Templars', Esoteric Theological Seminary, https://northernway.org/school/templars/2nd/MysteriesoftheTemplars.html, accessed 8 December 2021

Robertson, Janet, 'A knight was given tasks to do and became immortal' (audio recording), School of Scottish Studies Archive SA1981.86.A2, Tobar an Dualchais/Kist o Riches, https://www.tobarandualchais.co.uk/track/49867?l=en accessed 11 September 2021

Rowat, Alison, 'Secret Scotland with Susan Calman, series three, episode one', The Herald, *https://www.heraldscotland.com/news/18731872.secret-scotland-susan-calman-series-three-episode-one/*, accessed 8 December 2021

Sharp, Andrew 'Dalhousie Castle Ghosts' (storytelling video), Dalhousie Castle & Aqueous Spa Facebook Page, *https://fb.watch/bgqOWhET1h/*, accessed 19 January 2022

Unknown Author, 'About Moorfoot Community Council', Moorfoot Community Council, *https://moorfootcc.wordpress.com/*, accessed 23 May 2021

Unknown Author, 'Knights Templar: The Occult', Crusader History, *https://crusaderhistory.wordpress.com/2017/07/31/knights-templar-the-occult/*, accessed 15 June 2021

Unknown Author, 'Scottish crusaders and the Freemasonry link', The Herald, *https://www.heraldscotland.com/news/11930075.scottish-crusaders-and-the-freemasonry-link/*, accessed 24 July 2021

Vogan, Matthew, 'The Eventful Life of William Traill of Borthwick, Donegal and Maryland' (podcast), Scotland's Forgotten History, *https://scotlandsforgottenhistory.com/2020/09/04/the-eventful-life-of-william-traill-of-borthwick-donegal-and-maryland-sfh068/*, accessed 31 May 2021

Whiddon Green, Cynthia, 'Jocelyn, a Monk of Furness: The Life of Kentigern', Fordham University, *https://sourcebooks.fordham.edu/basis/jocelyn-lifeofkentigern.asp, accessed 8 December 2021*

Wilson, Heather, '5 Sites In Scotland That Are Connected To The Knights Templar', World Atlas, *https://www.worldatlas.com/articles/5-sites-in-scotland-that-are-connected-to-the-knights-templar.html, accessed 8 January 2022*

The Moorfoot Tales:
An Online Nature Therapy Programme

Eco-therapy (or Nature Therapy) is the practice of connecting with nature for our wellbeing and for the good of the planet, too. (People who care for nature are more inclined to take care of it.)

I have developed a series of online eco-therapy programmes that connect you with myth and your local landscape – including a programme based specifically on The Moorfoot Tales. You don't need to have any particular 'issues' going on, this is simply about connecting more deeply with nature through the power of story. I offer my full personal support throughout all programmes.

You can sign up for these programmes on my website, where you can also find out about my other eco-therapy projects including a free e-book and nature-based counselling.

www.naturetherapyonline.net

Printed in Great Britain
by Amazon